The Omen of the Mayan Astronaut: King Pakal V2

AUTHOR: RAFAEL ENRIQUE PARRAO LOPEZ

DEDICATION

This book is dedicated to:

My great-grandmother Petronila, a pure Mayan Indian, married to Manuel Parrao de la Gala of Portuguese origin, in the city of Tinún, Campeche.

 To my parents Rafael Parrao Pereyra and Margarita López y Pons, the first because he was always amazed by this great Mayan culture and who, like them, the number 13 followed him from his birth to his death and the second, my mother, for all his love and teachings since he was a child.

To my wife Marilú Suárez Peredo, for all her love, affection and fight for the happiness of our children: Eduardo Alejandro and Rafael David, from whom I continue to learn how to be a father.

To my niece Karla Patricia and Rubén, for their tireless work in preserving the delicate coral reefs, for protecting the wonders of the marine species of the Mexican Caribbean and for showing the world the great legacy of the Mayan culture.

Rafael Enrique Parrao López

CONTENT

FOREWORD

The history of humanity is filled with mysteries that challenge our understanding, immersing us in profound enigma. As a researcher of physical phenomena and nature, I have dedicated myself to unveiling these hidden secrets with foundations and scientific theories that can provide support and decipher the mysteries that persist through time. I share with you the revelations I have discovered.

In this, my first attempt at a science fiction novel, I invite you to embark on a fascinating journey that spans two pivotal moments in human history. Two events that will forever change our perception of the past and the future from a scientific perspective, yet tinged with elements of fiction.

The curtain of our story rises with the enigma that endures to this day: the manner or causes behind the disappearance of the Mayan culture, an ancient civilization that flourished in the Yucatán Peninsula and parts of Central America. For centuries, the fate of the Maya has intrigued archaeologists, historians, and all those seeking to understand the mysteries of the past, without any theory with substantial evidence explaining why or how they vanished suddenly.

In this narrative, presented in the form of a science fiction novel, I recount the story of a stela that becomes the key to solving this ancient puzzle. A stela commissioned by the Mayans, bearing secrets and encrypted messages that will reveal the truth behind the disappearance of this millennia-old culture. Additionally, following the clues left in three of the four preserved Codices—the Madrid, Paris, and Dresden Codices, along with the Grolier Codex from Mexico City—we will witness a discovery that will reshape our perspective on the Maya and their lost legacy.

However, the story doesn't stop there. A second moment unfolds before us—an urgent warning that transcends the barriers of time, alerting us to an imminent cataclysm. A massive asteroid threatens to collide with our planet in the year 2029, unleashing an apocalyptic catastrophe.

The key to deciphering this warning message is complemented by a stela discovered during the excavations of the Maya Train, an ambitious engineering project that aims to connect the destinies of the ancient Mayan cities. On this stela, written in a forgotten ancient language, lies the information that could save future civilizations from an uncertain fate.

Through the pages of this novel, we will witness the fascinating quest for answers, accompanying a group of bold and insightful researchers who delve into a labyrinth of ancient mysteries and imminent dangers. Every twist in the plot brings us closer to the hidden truth behind the Mayan enigmas and the fate looming over our own existence.

Prepare to embark on a journey filled with suspense, knowledge, and unimaginable perils. The secrets of the Maya and the warnings of the future will unfold before your eyes, guiding you through centuries of history and leading you towards an uncertain and bleak future if humanity does not unite.

Welcome to this thrilling adventure. The mystery is served, and the truth is about to be revealed.

Note: Any resemblance of the characters, organizations, or institutions in this novel to real persons, organizations, or institutions is purely coincidental.

CHAPTER 1: SELENA'S DESTINY

It was the year 1981, and the night sky sparkled with thousands of stars that piqued Selena's curiosity as she gazed at the sky by the sea. From a young age, she had felt a special connection with the cosmos and longed to unravel its deepest secrets. Her passion for observing the sky and diving would turn her into an exceptional woman.

Selena had brown hair and green eyes filled with determination, a brilliant mind since childhood. Her great-grandmother, a pure Mayan Indian, had instilled in her a love for ancestral roots and the wisdom of the ancient Mayans. Fascinated by their mysteries, Selena spent hours immersed in ancient books and studies on the prophecies and astronomical knowledge of this enigmatic civilization.

The Mayans, without modern technology, had been able to predict solar and lunar eclipses, even the transits of Venus, and that fascinated her. It was a scientific marvel that defied conventional logic. This cosmic foresight became Selena's primary goal. She was determined to discover how an ancient civilization had attained such celestial knowledge.

After completing her degree in Astronomy, Selena was recruited as a researcher at the country's most prestigious institute in her field. Here, surrounded by brilliant minds and cutting-edge equipment, Selena immersed herself in her work, but in her free time, she continued with her unwavering passion for Mayan culture. Over 30 years of her life were dedicated to unraveling the secrets of the cosmos, and unbeknownst to her, she was also approaching the revelation of one of the most transcendent mysteries of Mayan culture: their disappearance and the imminent danger of a cosmic collision with an asteroid.

Selena, now a distinguished and respected astronomer, stood on the threshold of a great adventure. She did not know that her tireless dedication and quest for answers would lead her to discover a truth that would change her life and the entire world. The threads of destiny were beginning to intertwine, and unknowingly, she would become a key player in solving a cosmic enigma that threatened the very existence of the planet.

With her eyes fixed on the firmament, Selena prepared for a journey that would transcend time and space, unveiling the mysteries of an ancient civilization and safeguarding the fate of humanity. Her steps would take her beyond the limits of the known, towards a future where the stars and the ancient Mayans converged for a singular purpose: unraveling the secrets of the universe and preserving life on Earth.

But what were the Mayans like in their heyday? Let's delve into this wonderful and mysterious culture and the fate of its remnants prior to the destiny reserved for Selena.

CHAPTER 2: THE ENIGMA OF THE MAYA TEMPLES

The sun ascended majestically over the Mayan land, illuminating with its golden radiance the four fabulous observation temples that stood as silent guardians of celestial mysteries. Ninety kines (90 Mayan days) remained until witnessing the majestic optical phenomenon of the spring equinox in the year 9.10.17.7.7 of the long count (read 650 A.D.), and K'inich Janaab' Pakal, the enigmatic Mayan king, ruled with wisdom and power over the vast territory of what is now the southeastern part of the Mexican Republic.

Mayan culture extended across a vast territory in what are now the states of Yucatán, Quintana Roo, Chiapas, and Tabasco in the Mexican Republic. In Central America, it occupied the current territories of Belize, Guatemala, Honduras, and El Salvador, with a documented history estimated to be over 5,137 years old (from 3114 B.C. to 2023 A.D.). As later confirmed, the true antiquity of the Maya civilization exceeds 10,400 years, making it the oldest culture on Earth.

Regarding their temples, four of them stood majestically in a wide area of astronomical observation preferred by Pakal, three on a mysterious island known as Mother Island situated off the town of Kankun, 80 kilometers offshore, and the fourth temple, located inland, 214 kilometers from the coast.

The Maya, skilled navigators, ventured in their boats into the crystal-clear waters of the Caribbean Sea to reach Mother Island, a sacred and privileged site for King Pakal's astronomical observations. The temples, built by a Mayan civilization over 10,400 Mayan years ago (two long counts), had been constructed with quartz, a crystalline and perplexing material for the Mayans of that time, as they seemed to radiate a mystical energy in perfect harmony with the celestial cycles they worshipped.

Each of these three temples on Mother Island had been built for the astronomical observation of a different celestial entity. The first pyramid was dedicated to the observation of the moon, the second pyramid to the observation of the planets Venus, Mars, Mercury, and Jupiter, and the third pyramid on the island was dedicated to the observation of comets and asteroids. The Mayans, masters of astronomy, had built these structures with mathematical precision, utilizing their profound knowledge of celestial movements to interpret the will of the gods.

The fourth pyramid, of more recent creation and located on the peninsula, was known as the Chichen Itza Pyramid, The Castle, or the Temple of Kukulkan. It stood inland on the plain, 214 kilometers from the coast. Unlike the other temples, this one was erected with enormous stone blocks, defying the force of time with its imposing presence. Its purpose was the observation of the Sun and its influence on the cycles of nature, which had an impact on planting and water supply cycles, vital for the life and destiny of the immense Mayan population, exceeding 300,000 people.

This pyramid presented various mathematical and astronomical analogies to symbolize their worship of the Sun. The ancient Mayans' ability to perform precise calculations and understand celestial phenomena was visually evident to any observer.

For instance, in the structure of its stairways: The pyramid had four sides, each with a staircase of 91 steps. By adding the steps from all four sides and the upper platform, which is the temple level, a total of 365 steps was reached, equaling the number of days in the Mayan solar year.

Solstices and equinoxes: During the spring and fall equinoxes, at sunset, a light and shadow phenomenon occurred on the pyramid. The sun cast shadows in the form of inverted triangles that joined the staircases and the snake heads at the base of the north side of the structure, creating an optical illusion of a descending serpent. This effect symbolized the descent of Kukulkan, the feathered serpent.

Venus: The position and movement of the planet Venus were important to the Maya. On the pyramid's facade, sculpted panels representing Venus and its phases could be observed. The Maya had a profound understanding of Venus cycles and related them to astronomical events and rituals.

Astronomical calculations: The pyramid's orientation was precisely aligned with the cardinal points, suggesting that the Maya had advanced knowledge of astronomy and could perform precise calculations to align their structures with celestial bodies.

These analogies and others, primarily of a mathematical and astronomical nature in the Chichen Itza pyramid, emphasized the importance and deep knowledge of time and natural cycles.

It was the golden age of Mayan culture, witnessing the grandeur and mysterious connection of their people with the cosmos through these temples. As the Mayan priestly caste, called Ah kin, explored the sky, their temples gained special relevance because the King could accurately predict the days when the sun or the moon "would momentarily go out" due to dissatisfaction with offerings. The people would then need to appease their anger through sacrifices and greater offerings to the Gods to calm them and pacify their impulses to destroy the Mayan people.

CHAPTER 3: THE HEAVENLY OMEN

It is night, and in the majestic Temple of Chichen Itza, whose meaning in the Mayan language is "at the edge of the well where the Wise Ones of the Water live," the Mayan priests surround King Pakal with serious and concerned faces. The King had arrived after a long journey from Palenque to be informed about the new findings his priests had for him after extended observations. During his stay in the temple, they have precisely calculated a series of astronomical events. However, a recent discovery has put the Mayan sages on high alert.

King Pakal listens attentively as the priests inform him of the discovery of three asteroids whose trajectories threaten the Mayan civilization. One of them is heading directly towards the triple temple on Mother Island, while the largest and brightest, referred to as Bolon Yokte in honor of the God of War, and its smaller companion, will pass dangerously close but on a very distant date.

The news shakes the king and his court. The fate of their kingdom and the astronomical wonders built by their ancestors ten thousand years before any other culture is at stake. Aware of the importance of celestial phenomena and their influence on the fate of his civilization, Pakal summons his priests for a desperate search for answers.

The Mayan sages delve into the ancient Codices of their ancestors in search of clues that can unravel the enigma of the asteroids and their collision trajectory but find no answers. Tension rises among the Mayan priests as King Pakal ventures into the darkness of the jungle, following paths marked by the stars and ancestral inscriptions, trying to find a solution.

Using their wisdom and knowledge, the priests travel to Mother Island and decipher the hidden prophecies in the carvings of the pyramids there. They unravel a chilling message: the encoded messages on the temple walls of Mother Island resemble an apocalyptic cosmic event that occurred 3764 years ago, precisely on August 11, 3114 B.C. – the year in which the 13th Baktun of the long count was completed, even though their system is vigesimal, and they should wait until the end of the twentieth Baktun to complete it. They decide to adopt the notion that the long count concludes at the end of the 13th Baktun, marking it as an apocalyptic date.

Perplexed, Pakal asks his priests what cyclical apocalyptic event is recorded, and the priests clarify that, according to the inscriptions on the temples of Mother Island, at the end of the 13th Baktun, the planet passes through a belt of asteroids with a high likelihood of causing the end of the Mayan world. That's why their ancestors recorded only 13 Baktuns instead of the 20 in their mathematical system, to alert future generations. Due to this, ancient priests carved the cosmic event in stone and recommended recording anything useful for future generations that might survive.

Time becomes a relentless enemy for King Pakal as the priest's race against the clock to find a solution. Their determination strengthens as each piece of the astronomical puzzle falls into place, but knowledge alone is not enough; bold actions and a profound understanding of the mysteries of the universe are required.

CHAPTER 4: THE CLOCK OF DESTINY

King Pakal, aware of the imminent threat looming over his kingdom, calls for an urgent meeting with his priests at the Temple of Chichen Itza. Determination shines in his eyes as he instructs the wise men to precisely calculate the date and location where the asteroids will impact the Earth.

The priests, armed with their extensive mathematical and astronomical knowledge, delve into intricate calculations to determine the fate of the asteroids. With certainty in their voices, they inform the king that the largest asteroid will impact in just 90 kines (90 days) off the coasts of Kankun on 9.10.17.7.7 (March 21, 650 A.D.). A shiver runs down the spine of everyone present as they visualize the devastation that this cosmic event could unleash on Mother Island and the Mayan peninsula.

But that's not all; the priests also announce that two more asteroids, one very large and another smaller, will impact in the distant future near the Temple of Chichen Itza, in the year of the long count 13.0.16.15.6. The king and the priests grasp the magnitude of what this means: they could warn future Mayan generations that manage to survive the impending cosmic event and thus preserve Maya culture over time, just as their predecessors did.

The tension in the air is palpable as the Mayan priests confront the unavoidable reality of an imminent disaster. Pakal, driven by his profound love for his people and his passion for astronomy, ventures into an uncertain path but one filled with hope. He is confident that the future civilization and its advancements will find a solution.

The race against time to find a solution that can save their kingdom and protect future generations is inexorable. The priests immerse themselves in a frenzy of activities, revisiting their observations and calculations, searching for any clues that could lead to a possible error and their salvation.

Meanwhile, time advances relentlessly toward the fateful date. The Mayan people will undoubtedly face challenges and setbacks; the obstacles seem insurmountable, and only determination and the will to fight against adversities will enable the entire community to move forward.

CHAPTER 5: THE EXODUS TO PALENQUE

Despite their resignation and misfortune, King Pakal convenes a meeting in the Temple of Chichen Itza with his priests. The devastating news must be shared; there is no way to avoid the impact of the largest asteroid that inexorably approaches the Mayan kingdom.

The atmosphere is filled with sadness and desperation as Pakal, with a firm yet sorrowful voice, orders his priests to immediately alert the people and initiate the evacuation. There is no time to lose, and the priority is to safeguard the lives of his beloved people. He will stay for a few days with his chief priests to plan how to alert future Mayan generations that may survive the cosmic apocalypse.

Dark and turbulent times were upon them. The once glorious Mayan people in Chichen Itza are forced to abandon their beloved home and embark on a journey full of hardships towards a new destination: Palenque. The adverse circumstances and challenges of this journey would leave a deep mark on the souls of those brave Mayans.

The exodus began in the middle of the night, as the moon hid behind the shadows of the temples. Mayan families, in a final farewell to their ancestral city, walked through streets that were once vibrant with life and rituals but now lay deserted and silent. Hearts were filled with sadness as they left behind their homes, the majestic pyramids, and the sacred sanctuaries.

The caravan of the Mayans, carrying their most precious belongings and the memories of past generations, ventured into the vast jungle, where the murmur of the trees and the songs of the birds mingled with their sighs of nostalgia. The dense and lush vegetation became an obstacle, intertwining its branches as if to halt their progress.

The paths were dangerous and unknown. The Mayans had to face steep terrain, rushing rivers, and treacherous swamps. Thirst and hunger seized them as they penetrated deeper into the unforgiving jungle. Many fell ill and weakened, unable to withstand the harsh conditions of the journey.

The journey was fraught with threats. Wild beasts lurked in the darkness, waiting for their chance to attack. Furious storms swept through the makeshift camps, leaving destruction and despair in their wake. Uncertainty and fear clung to their hearts as the road stretched beyond imagination.

But despite it all, the Mayans found strength in their spirit and their deep connection with nature. They celebrated rituals to honor their gods, seeking their protection and guidance amid adversity. The elders shared stories of resilience and bravery, reminding everyone of the greatness of their civilization.

Finally, after countless days of suffering and sacrifice, they arrived in Palenque, the land that offered them the hope of a new beginning. Although the pain and sadness for what they had left behind lingered in their hearts, they clung to the promise of rebuilding and keeping their culture alive.

Meanwhile, in Chichen Itza, King Pakal has perfected his plan, and a new command emerges from his lips. Determined, he entrusts them with the task of writing in three Royal Codices the account of the imminent astronomical event and the one that is yet to come. It is vital that future generations and the descendants who manage to survive be alert and prepared for another catastrophic event, but will the Codices withstand the cosmic event, and if so, the inexorable deterioration of time?

The priests immerse themselves in a task of historical significance. With trembling yet steady hands, they begin to record in their Codices the account of the impact of the first asteroid about to fall on their kingdom, indicating the date and location of the fateful event that is about to occur: Kankun 9.10.17.7.7 (March 21, 650 AD)

.

CHAPTER 6: ANCESTRAL TESTIMONY

In the midst of the chaos and uncertainty surrounding the Maya kingdom, King Pakal realizes that the impact of the first asteroid could erase the remnants of the Codices forever. Aware of the importance of preserving ancestral knowledge, he makes a second bold and transcendent decision.

King Pakal summons his priests and instructs them to preserve the valuable information for posterity. He orders that the date of the fateful event, destined to occur in the future, be inscribed on a large stone stela. Since the astronomical information required to decipher the event is extensive and it would be impossible to carve all of it in stone, he directs them to specify the remaining details in three Royal Codices that they must guard with their lives.

The stone stela will consist of two monoliths for ease of transportation. One of them will highlight the most crucial aspect the impending catastrophic event if nothing is done: "The End of the Maya World" and its date. The second monolith will provide details about the cause that will trigger it.

Pakal orders them to engrave the fateful date on the stela before the cosmic event, so that they may be alerted in advance and can prevent it by all means available in their era. The sacred stela should not be large but lightweight, allowing it to be transported to the remote Temple of Palenque and withstand the apocalyptic event.

King Pakal instructs them as follows:

"The three Royal Codices will bear the character of the Royal Codex, meaning they will be engraved with the seal of King Pakal. They will be safeguarded in Palenque and permanently guarded from generation to generation by the Itza's. They are to provide the following information:

The first Royal Codex: The cause, the imminent fall of the three asteroids. They must provide the current astronomical position of Venus, Mars, Jupiter, Saturn, and the brightest celestial bodies to allow future generations to identify, through progressive mathematical calculations of these positions, which asteroids will collide."

The second Royal Codex: The location of the asteroids. They must provide the current astronomical position with respect to constellations and the most visible planets at the observation date, along with their orbital period relative to the sun, enabling the extrapolation of their future positions based on the planets' locations.

Third Royal Codex: The dates of the collision of the three asteroids with the planet. They must provide the astronomical position of the brightest planets and celestial bodies on the day of the collision, along with the precise date."

King Pakal adds, "If any additional information, after the first collision, becomes necessary to determine the impact of the remaining two asteroids in the future, my eldest surviving descendant shall write it in a fourth Codex. This Codex will be left beside me in the Sacred Temple that they will erect for me. From there, I will journey in my vessel to the underworld to warn you again in the future of this apocalypse. The sign of my return will be on the 13.10.0.17.9 day when Kukulkan descends in Chichen Itza, and the entire city darkens, and a golden ring covers the Sun God (October 14, 2023)."

The news evokes both hope and fear among the priests. The task of gathering so much data and carving such a crucial testimony in stone involves a titanic effort, and the challenge of conveying the minimal elements necessary for future understanding is even greater.

With meticulousness and skill, the Maya priests embark on the task of carving the sacred stela and writing the Royal Codices. Every stroke and symbol must be precise, conveying the message of the impending cosmic disaster looming over them. The wise Maya know that time is against them, while King Pakal watches the progress of the task with a mix of anguish and determination.

The Maya priests live in the tension between the time they have left and the preservation of knowledge. Each chisel strike is an act of resistance against the impending devastation, as the clock inexorably ticks towards the fateful encounter with the asteroid.

CHAPTER 7: THE LOST STELE

Having engraved in stone the transcendent astronomical event about to occur and what will happen to those who survive from the Maya people in 1379 years, King Pakal prepares to ensure that the sacred stela, composed of two monoliths, is swiftly but carefully transported to the Temple of Palenque. Aware of the incalculable value of this recorded testimony, he entrusts his best messengers to carry out this crucial mission.

The messengers, brave and resilient men, set out with the sacred stela on a journey laden with responsibility. Their goal is to traverse the intricate jungle that separates Chichen Itza from Palenque. However, destiny has an unexpected challenge in store for them.

Amidst the dense jungle, the insurgent tribes that have defied Pakal's rule lurk in the shadows. As if aware of the value held by the sacred stela, they launch an attack, thirsty for power and riches. The struggle is fierce and ruthless, a battle between the preservation of knowledge and the greed of the rebels turns bloody.

In the midst of the fierce encounter, the sacred stela falls on a mountainside, and the monoliths separate, each falling in different places and getting lost in the density of the jungle, right in the final stretch towards Palenque. The messengers, wounded and defeated, flee back to Chichen Itza with the devastating news. No one knows the final fate of the sacred stela, and a mystery shrouds the legacy that Pakal sought to preserve.

The Maya people plunge into despair and uncertainty surrounding the disappearance of the sacred stela. Consumed by frustration and powerlessness, Pakal wonders if someday the testimony engraved in stone will be found.

Pakal orders the dispatch of a significant group of warriors to the area of the attack, but the Maya's efforts to recover the lost object become relentless, exploring the jungle inch by inch in the hope of locating it, but with fruitless results.

CHAPTER 8: THE FLIGHT TOWARDS PALENQUE

With the imminent fate of the first impact, King Pakal faces a difficult but necessary decision. Aware that nothing can be done to prevent the cataclysm, he prepares to lead the few remaining inhabitants of the village who still resist leaving the area to Palenque, his birthplace and an apparently secure refuge.

The news of the impending impact spreads quickly among the Maya, filling their hearts with fear and anguish. However, Pakal emerges as a brave and determined leader, urging his people to maintain hope and trust that they will reach Palenque safely.

With the remaining Maya population leaving their homes and belongings in search of a chance to survive, Pakal begins the long journey. The road to Palenque is fraught with challenges, with dangers lurking at every moment in the jungle, compounded by the uncertainty of the future weighing on them.

While the Mayan people advance towards Palenque, the emotions and ties of friendship between tribes in the area that see large areas liberated become a crisis, very few try to return distrusting the certainty of the wise astronomers, the vast majority, aware of their great mathematical and astronomical wisdom, have already arrived and await their King who accompanies the oldest and most defenseless. The long journey highlights the immense sacrifice that the entire people and each individual must make to protect their loved ones and ensure the survival of their cultural legacy. As the group ventures into the jungle and approaches Palenque, they encounter various obstacles and surprising encounters. Relationships are put to the test, and the vulnerable elderly discover new strengths and hidden abilities within themselves, thanks to the encouragement of their King who motivates them not to falter.

CHAPTER 9: THE IMPENDING DOOM

Two long months have passed since King Pakal and his people left the Mother Island and the plains of Chichen Itza, and the final destination has finally arrived. The precise calculations of the Maya priests have come true, and the massive asteroid, with a diameter of over 500 meters, inexorably approaches the earth.

Tension hangs over the Maya kingdom as the sky slowly darkens, and warning signs become increasingly evident. The news of the imminent impact spreads like wildfire among the people, generating fear and desperation.

In the heart of the night, when the stars twinkle over the limestone peninsula, suddenly a deafening roar cuts through the air, culminating in a massive explosion.

The scorched asteroid falls just 80 kilometers off the coast of Cancun, splitting the peninsula in two and unleashing a storm of chaos and destruction.

The fiery fragments of the asteroid plummet from the sky, transforming into fireballs that fall in all directions. The earth trembles violently and cracks open upon impact, giving rise to enormous cavities rapidly filled with crystalline water. These deep abysses will become massive cenotes, silent witnesses to the cataclysm shaking the region.

The thunderous roar echoes in the ears of the survivors as they helplessly watch the immense part of the peninsula sink into the tumultuous sea. The three majestic pyramids of the mother island, silent witnesses to the splendor of the ancient Mayan kings, disappear beneath the turbulent waters, taking with them the secrets and greatness of an entire civilization.

In the midst of darkness and confusion, the few Mayas who did not evacuate cling to hope and struggle to survive, but all perish by drowning. Moments of anguish and bravery unfold among the Maya people as they confront the destruction of their homes and the loss of their cultural legacy.

CHAPTER 10: THE WRATH OF THE SEA

The entire population plunges into chaos and desolation following the impact of the asteroid and the collapse of the Mayan peninsula. As the massive island of the Maya kingdom sinks into the sea, a new and devastating phenomenon is unleashed: a giant tsunami.

The roar of the ocean is heard from afar as the sea waters surge towards the land, forming an immense wave over 40 meters high that rises with unrestrained fury. Coastal communities are the first to be swept away by the powerful current, with no time to escape the impending tragedy.

The tsunami advances mercilessly, engulfing everything in its path. Trees, animals, rocks, and humans are swept away by the relentless force of the waters. Small towns that underestimated the calculations of the Maya priests and did not manage to evacuate are erased from the face of the peninsula, while the Mayan Island submerges into an ocean reclaiming its territory.

Even the great pyramid of Chichen Itza, though located 200 kilometers inland and far from the coast, does not escape the wrath of the unleashed sea. The turbulent water manages to strike two of its sides with ferocity—those facing the coast—hurling debris and remnants in its wake. The staircases for ascent on the sides of the pyramid facing the onslaught of the waves from its base to its pinnacle partially crumble under the onslaught, succumbing to the destructive force of the tsunami.

Side 1 of the pyramid facing the Caribbean Sea, showing the damages caused by the tsunami.

Side 2 of the pyramid facing the Caribbean Sea, showing the damages caused by the tsunami.

However, as an act of resistance and pride, the sides opposite to the coast of the pyramid, untouched by the tsunami, remain steadfast and standing without apparent destruction. Despite the relentless onslaught of the water, these ancient stone structures refuse to fall, defying the fury of the sea and becoming symbols of the resilience of the Maya people.

Sides of the pyramid opposite to the sea, not damaged by the tsunami.

CHAPTER 11: THE SUBMERGED KINGDOM

Despite evacuation efforts, some Maya perish beneath the relentless waves, taking with them thousands of square kilometers of remnants of an ancient astronomical culture. The cataclysm unleashed by the tsunami leaves a trail of destruction and desolation in its wake. The overwhelming force of water, mud, and debris carries away the traces of a great culture that once flourished in the Maya peninsula. Three of its pyramids, temples, and observatories on the mother island sink into the ocean abyss, devoured by the turbulent waters.

In the midst of this tragedy and sorrow, King Pakal, a lover of astronomy and a wise ruler, succumbs to the diseases that arise and passes away a few days later at the age of 68. His departure marks the end of an era and leaves a profound void in the heart of the Maya people. To pay him eternal homage, Maya priests come together to build a funerary structure that will be a sacred place destined to venerate his memory for centuries to come.

In tribute to him, the Maya erect the Temple of the Inscriptions, an imposing monument that houses a sarcophagus containing the remains of King Pakal and testimonies of his greatness. The temple stands not only as a ceremonial center but also as a sacred burial place and sanctuary for the Maya King.

In this temple, the Maya deposited the legacy of their great leader, protecting his memory and hoping that in the future, it could be discovered, and his story revealed.

It would take over twelve hundred years for the tomb of King Pakal to be discovered. In 1949, archaeologist Alberto Ruz Lhuillier found twelve symmetrical holes in a slab on the top of the Temple of the Inscriptions, which seemed to have been made to support the ruler's throne. Upon realizing that there was a hollow space under this slab, he began to dig and found the steps of the internal staircase of the pyramid, whose passage was completely blocked. On June 15, 1952, after removing tons of stone and debris, the team of archaeologists managed to penetrate the mortuary chamber, measuring 7.00 m long by 3.73 m wide, which was covered in stalagmites and stalactites.

The main lid, carved in high relief and weighing seven tons, was lifted with the help of hydraulic jacks, and at the bottom of the sarcophagus, a secondary fish-shaped lid was found. Finally, upon opening this second lid, King Pakal's skeleton was discovered, covered in cinnabar and surrounded by numerous ornaments and jade beads. On November 27, 1952, Ruz Lhuillier made the public announcement of this discovery.

For those Maya priests, the king was nothing less than a guide, even illuminated, and they dedicated themselves to immortalizing the image of Pakal. Both the sarcophagus, the lid covering it, and the walls of the crypt were decorated with reliefs alluding to Pakal's royal genealogy and references to the creation myths of Maya culture.

CHAPTER 12: IN SEARCH OF THE LOST LEGACY

Following the death of King Pakal and aware of the vital importance of preserving the astronomical discovery and his strong desire to alert future generations, the Maya priests embark on a challenging and transcendent mission: to find the monoliths that make up the sacred stele.

Guided by the conviction instilled in them by King Pakal, that the knowledge contained in the Codices and the stele can alert and save the Maya people in the future, the priests of Chichen Itza form the Itza's Lodge. This Lodge's mission is to guard the precious Codices, transmit the ancestral wisdom and secrets encapsulated in the cosmos from parents to children, and, above all, to alert future generations of the second and third asteroids that will fall on the Maya peninsula.

The Itza's, as guardians of the lost legacy, commit to protecting and preserving these treasures for future generations. With unwavering determination, they explore the lands that were once the Maya kingdom, venturing into the lush jungle and facing challenges that stand in their way.

The search for the lost sacred stele becomes a fascinating odyssey full of mysteries. The priests delve into the jungle, following clues and signs left by their ancient predecessors. As they progress, they discover coded hints in Maya inscriptions and the architecture of forgotten temples.

The Itza's Lodge becomes a brotherhood dedicated to knowledge, wisdom, and the preservation of collective memory. The priests, infused with tireless passion, seek to unravel the mysteries left by their ancestors, convinced that the lost stele holds the key to unveiling the fate of their civilization.

Amidst the jungle, surrounded by lush and enigmatic nature, the Itza's face hidden dangers and supernatural challenges. However, their determination and ancestral knowledge guide them at every step, bringing them closer to the long-awaited discovery.

CHAPTER 13: THE FLEETING ENCOUNTER

It's been almost a millennium, and the year is 1519, when the imposing figure of Hernán Cortés de Monroy y Pizarro Altamirano is planning to invade the Yucatán Peninsula and conquer it. With a select group of five hundred and fifty men and sixteen valuable horses, Cortés will embark on a journey into the unknown, towards rich and dangerous lands that promise a great adventure.

Catalina Suárez Marcayda, Hernán Cortés's first wife, tries to convince him not to undertake the journey until he assembles a larger army on the island called Cuba. However, Cortés dismisses her suggestion and persuades her to stay on the island with her sister Constanza Suárez Marcayda (my wife's twenty-ninth great-grandmother) for her safety until his return from the daring expedition, as he does not want to endanger her with the natives of the continent.

Before landing in Yucatán, Cortés disembarks on the island of Cozumel, where he encounters one of his men, Alvarado, who had advanced part of the expedition. However, the meeting is not entirely auspicious, as Alvarado has disobeyed Cortés's orders by interfering in a native village and committing acts that go against winning the friendship and favor of the natives.

Cortés, with his sharp gaze and strategic mind, reprimands Alvarado for his imprudence. He knows that, to succeed in this unknown land, it is crucial to gain the trust and respect of the natives, establish alliances, and understand their customs and beliefs. Therefore, he removes him from that mission and places Diego Velázquez in charge, who, with respect, good treatment, and the promise to protect them from the tribes that are accustomed to attacking and robbing them, manages to enlist the natives in Hernán Cortés's journey, guiding them toward the empire of the great Tenochtitlan.

With a steady and determined pace, Cortés ventures into the jungles of Yucatán, facing the challenges of the jungle, the inclemency of the weather, and internal tensions within his own expedition. As they advance, they encounter Maya tribes, whose eyes fill with amazement and fear at the presence of the Spaniards and their powerful horses.

Hernán Cortés and his expedition find themselves at a crucial point in the conquest of new lands for Spain. In their eagerness to explore these mysterious lands and conquer their riches, Cortés and his people face a cultural clash and the need to establish relationships of respect and understanding with the customs and traditions of the natives, as they far outnumber the Spanish forces.

CHAPTER 14: THE MEETING OF BELIEFS

During their passage through Cozumel, even though no sacrifices are carried out in these ceremonies, Cortés and his men are not entirely pleased. They observe the practices closely and feel challenged in their own beliefs and convictions. Although they had heard of the Maya rituals, witnessing them in person generates a certain discomfort and bewilderment.

Faced with this situation, the Spaniards engage in conversations with the Maya priests and the local chief. Seeking to win their favor and establish a connection, Cortés presents them with a wooden cross and an image of the Virgin, hoping that they would be objects of prayers. However, the priests and native leaders reject them and assure them that their gods are not evil, and they had even been warned about the imminent destruction that was approaching. They firmly declare their intention to maintain their worship of their ancestral deities.

The ancient Maya beliefs stood as a formidable challenge for the Spanish conquistadors. While the conquerors arrived with the mission of imposing their faith and replacing the Maya idols with the cross and the image of the Virgin, they encountered fierce resistance from the natives.

Rooted in centuries of traditions and rituals, the Maya saw their gods and idols as fundamental to their daily lives and their connection to the divine. Each temple and sanctuary held the essence of their spirituality, conveyed through statues and sacred representations. For them, the proposed change by the Spaniards was a desecration of their worldview and a direct attack on their cultural identity.

However, the Spanish conquerors were not easily dissuaded. Driven by their determination and religious fervor, they took the initiative and decided to confront the challenge head-on. In the defiant gaze of the natives, the Spaniards advanced towards the sacred Maya temples, carrying Christian symbols in their hands.

In a bold act, they began to topple the Maya idols that had remained motionless for centuries. The stone statues, intricately carved and revered for generations, fell to the ground shattered. Wood and jade, once objects of reverence, now turned into scattered debris.

While the Spaniards wielded their hammers and raised their crosses high, the natives looked on with a mix of desperation and anger. Each blow resonated as an affront to their deepest beliefs and as an affront to their very existence. The sound of the impact intertwined with cries and lamentations, forming a cacophony that seemed to challenge the very universe itself.

But despite the Spanish attempt to suppress and replace Maya beliefs, the essence of resistance persisted. Although the physical idols had been destroyed, the fire of Maya faith burned deep within their hearts. Secret ceremonies and forbidden rituals continued in the shadows, keeping alive the flame of their cultural and spiritual heritage.

In this encounter between two worlds, determination and stubbornness clashed in a battle of ideologies. The Spaniards, driven by their faith, sought to extend the boundaries of Christianity. The

Maya, rooted in their ancestral identity, fought to preserve their traditions and beliefs.

Ultimately, this confrontation not only defined the fate of Maya temples but would leave an indelible mark on the history of America. Through destruction and resistance, the foundations for the rich and complex cultural blend that would define the region to this day were forged.

CHAPTER 15: THE DISPUTE OF THE CODES

After witnessing the Maya ceremonies and establishing contact with the native leaders, Bishop Diego de Landa proposes a drastic measure to Hernán Cortés: the burning of all Maya writings and codices. His intention is to eliminate any trace of the ancient religion to facilitate the evangelization of the natives.

Upon learning of this, the Itza's Lodge, aware of the importance that the codices hold regarding the end of the Maya world in the future, strongly oppose this idea and put up a fierce defense against the Spaniards. They argue that these texts contain relevant and valuable information for the future, not only for the Maya but even for the Spaniards themselves, and they plead to speak with Hernán Cortés. Intrigued by this mysterious claim, Cortés attentively listens to the astronomical arguments of the great Master of the Itza's, who narrates the cosmic event that occurred five hundred years ago. Cortés decides not to destroy the three codices referred to by the Itza's as Royal Codices, agreeing to safeguard them and bring them as a gift to King Charles I of Spain and V of the Holy Roman Empire of Spain, whom we will henceforth refer to as Charles V.

Although Cortés shows some openness to safeguarding these writings, he does not display the same compassion toward the rest of the written remnants about the Maya gods and orders the Franciscan friar Diego de Landa to decide what to do with them. Friar Diego de Landa, determined to evangelize the natives, gives the order, and the soldiers proceed to destroy all written documents related to the ancient religion, aiming to impose the Christian religion on the Maya people.

Ironically, this same friar included in his reports to Spain a book titled "Relation de las cosas de Yucatán" ("Account of the Things of Yucatán"), in which he describes a rudimentary alphabet created with the help of the indigenous people of the area. He assigned one or more Maya signs equivalent to each letter of the Spanish alphabet. Although the Maya did not have a proper alphabet, this book contributed 200 years later to deciphering Maya writing composed of more than 800 glyphs in the Sacred Codices.

CHAPTYER 16: THE MYSTERY LOCKED IN

The wind blew forcefully as the waves battered the hull of the ship sailing across the Atlantic. Diego Peredo y Acuña, with a racing heart, clung to the helm while following Hernán Cortés's orders to the letter. The mission's destination was clear: return to Spain in secret, carrying with them the three Royal Codices and news of the fabulous treasures and riches in the newly conquered lands.

In the midst of the journey, a devastating storm threatened to sink the ship. Lightning illuminated the dark sky, while monstrous waves challenged the vessel's resilience. However, with tenacity and skill, Diego Peredo managed to navigate the danger and keep his valuable cargo afloat.

Finally, the ship arrived in Spain, and Diego hastened to present the treasures and Codices to King Charles V. In the royal hall, the monarch waited impatiently, eager to learn the details of the conquered riches and Maya wonders.

With solemnity, Diego presented fifty quintals overflowing with gold, silver, and jade as an offering to the king. Then, he unveiled the three Maya Codices, carefully wrapped, and began narrating to the monarch the astonishing achievements of the Maya civilization and the fierceness with which they defended these Codices.

With passionate words, he described the fabulous temples and cities they had conquered in the name of Charles V. He mentioned the architectural greatness of their temples and pyramids and the Maya's advancements in mathematics and astronomy. Every detail painted a fascinating picture of a lost civilization that had reached an impressive level of knowledge.

Amazed by the treasures and wealth that would come to his kingdom, King Charles V granted Cortés the title of Conqueror of New Spain and ordered Diego to return reinforced with 300 Spaniards, horses, and supplies.

Diego Peredo returned excitedly to Yucatán, making a stop in Cuba to marry Constanza Suárez, whom he loved and promised to return to after fulfilling Cortés's mandate. From this marriage, Diego Suárez Peredo was born, preserving his mother's surname due to the significant weight of being the sister-in-law of the Conqueror's wife. He would later receive the title of Count of the Valley of Orizaba, unaware that one of his future descendants in the 20th century would be married to Enrique, Selena's brother, the astronomer who would play a key role in deciphering the Maya enigma guarded in the Royal Codices and the enormous task of saving humanity.

Meanwhile, in Spain, intrigued by the magnitude of the discoveries, King Charles V decided to examine the Codices himself. He unrolled one of them, and his eyes met the enigmatic Maya glyphs. A strange mixture of astonishment and confusion reflected on his face. Unable to decipher their meaning, he decided to rely on the wisdom of the scholars at court.

Aware of the importance of the Codices, King Charles V ordered them to be safeguarded in the royal library. However, to ensure their protection and prevent them from falling into the wrong hands, he decided to hide them in three separate and secret locations, far from prying eyes.

The monarch was unaware that destiny would play an unexpected role in preserving these treasures. In future invasions and conflicts, Spain would lose two of the three precious Codices, not knowing that these would end up in the hands of other nations and that Maya knowledge would transcend borders. Meanwhile, in the royal library, the remaining Codex would patiently await its historic moment in the unveiling of the enigma it holds.

CHAPTER 17: THE RESCUE OF THE CODEX

The year was 1739, and Johann Christian Götze, a renowned German theologian and librarian, found himself immersed in a fascinating journey through Italy and Austria. During his travels, a chance encounter would change his life and leave an indelible mark on the history of Maya knowledge.

While exploring the wonders that European culture had to offer, Götze had the opportunity to meet a Viennese aristocrat. This man, aware of Götze's passion for manuscripts and antiquities, offered him something that immediately captured his attention: a book from an ancient culture with unknown characters and hieroglyphic figures.

The German librarian accepted the offer with amazement and gratitude, unaware of the importance of that manuscript in his hands. In his work titled "Die Merckwürdigkeiten der Königliche Bibliotheck zu Dreßden" ("The Wonders of the Royal Library of Dresden"), he described his discovery as follows: "A Mexican book with unknown characters and hieroglyphic figures written on both sides, and painted with all kinds of colors, in an elongated octavo, carefully folded in folds or sheets, 39 together, extending along the unload in six cubits."

Unbeknownst to him, Johann Christian Götze was rescuing one of the precious Maya Codices, which, by the whims of fate, one of the subjects of the King of Spain of Viennese origin had extracted from the Royal Library when removed from his position. His experience as a librarian indicated the importance of protecting and preserving that cultural treasure.

With caution and knowledge, Götze brought the Codex to the Library of Saxony in Dresden, Germany. There, in the sanctuary of knowledge, he safeguarded the Maya manuscript, unaware of the significance it would have in the history of ancient civilization.

Years passed, and the Maya Codex remained secure in the library. However, its content and meaning remained an enigma to the academic world. Scholars and researchers longed to decipher the secrets locked in those hieroglyphs, but the answers resisted revealing themselves.

Johann Christian Götze's serendipitous discovery was a crucial step in preserving Maya wisdom. His dedication as a librarian and his love for manuscripts allowed this Codex to reach the right hands. Now, it was only a matter of time before scholars and experts in ancient languages uncovered the true meaning of this Maya treasure, unraveling the mysteries that had intrigued entire generations.

CHAPTER 18: THE MAYAN ENIGMS AND THE DECODERS

The year was 1807, and Napoleon's shadow covered the Iberian Peninsula. Spain, initially an ally of France, found itself betrayed when French troops invaded its territory. The king of Spain was deposed, destabilizing the monarchical system and causing a power crisis throughout the Hispanic world.

Joseph Bonaparte, Napoleon's brother, was crowned as the new Spanish monarch, taking the title of Joseph I. Meanwhile, the legitimate king, Ferdinand VII, and his father remained prisoners in France, adding even more tension and confusion to the Spanish empire.

As Spain was invaded by Napoleon and French troops encroached into Portugal to seize that country as well, Spaniards and Portuguese fled to the coast of Lisbon to escape the massacre.

In the port of Lisbon, moored and ready to set sail as usual, was a Schooner waited named "El Republicano," owned by Jacinto, a merchant who frequently traded Castilian wax with the salt of New Spain. That afternoon, and fleeing from the French invasion, one of his best friends, Manuel, a tall, single young man with enormous mustaches, came to visit him and made a huge request:

Manuel: "Jacinto, we have been great friends and business partners in the trade of wax and salt for many years, but now I need to ask you a huge favor. The French troops, as you know, have already invaded Spain and are now entering Portugal, and our families are in danger. I have heard that you are about to disembark, and I would like to ask you a massive favor—to allow me, my parents, and my two brothers to escape with you and your family to New Spain; otherwise, I am sure they will kill us while trying to take over the salt warehouses we have."

Jacinto: "We have always faced everything together, Manuel. Hurry and bring your belongings and family; we set sail in the evening for the port of Campeche in New Spain."

On that cold morning of December 5, 1807, "El Republicano" would depart from the port of Lisbon, with Manuel unaware that these new lands had reserved for him the experience of falling in love with an intelligent and beautiful young woman of Maya origin named Petronila Herrera. She would later become the great-grandmother of the astronomer who would play a key role in deciphering the mystery of Pakal's sacred stele.

Brigantine Schooner El Republicano

Meanwhile, in Spain and amidst political uncertainty, José Bonaparte learned of the fascination the Mayan Codices sent by Cortés had aroused in the King of Spain. With great interest, he ordered them to be presented to him, not knowing how many were in the kingdom, so he only received one of them. The second Codex had been lost since 1739 in the Royal Library of Dresden. However, the Spanish subjects kept the existence of the third Codex, the largest and most valuable of all, a secret in the city of Madrid.

Impressed by the Codex in his possession, José Bonaparte decided to send it as a gift to his brother Napoleon. The French emperor, intrigued by this ancient Mayan work, sent it to the national museum of France for study and analysis by French experts.

The 1830s brought a new chapter in the history of the Mayan Codices. Constantine Samuel Rafinesque-Smaltz, a man of multicultural origin born in Turkey, showed great interest in the Dresden Codex. This scholar, the son of a French father and a German mother, devoted his life to the study and search for answers in the enigmatic Mayan glyphs.

In his journal "Atlantic Journal and Friend of Knowledge," published in the United States, Constantine shared his findings and discoveries about Mayan writing. He sent letters to his contemporary Jean François Champollion, who was immersed in the challenge of deciphering Egyptian hieroglyphs, exposing his ideas about Mayan writing.

With the limited information available at that time about Palenque and the pages of the Dresden Codex previously published by Alexander Von Humboldt, Constantine Samuel Rafinesque-Smaltz managed to be the first to unravel the values of bars and dots in the Mayan numbering system.

As the years passed, Mayan mysteries began to slowly unfold thanks to the valuable work of scholars like Constantine. His efforts, along with those of other academics and experts in ancient languages, paved the way for the decipherment of ancient Mayan writing and the understanding of their rich culture and mathematical knowledge.

CHAPTER 19: THE ENIGMS OF THE DRESDEN CODEX

In the depths of the Royal Library of Saxony in Dresden, Germany, librarian Ernest Förstemann embarked on an archaeological quest through the treasures stored on its shelves. Among old scrolls and manuscripts, his eyes fell upon an ancient and enigmatic Codex: the Dresden Codex.

The pre-Hispanic appearance of the Codex immediately captured Förstemann's attention. He knew he was facing an invaluable treasure, a window into the ancient Mayan civilization. Determined to unravel its meaning, he immersed himself in a deep study, leveraging the findings of Constantine Samuel Rafinesque-Smaltz and other experts.

Förstemann dedicated countless hours to deciphering the complex Mayan glyphs and made a startling discovery: the Long Count. This uninterrupted record dated back to the creation of the Mayan universe on 4 Ajaw 8 Kumku, corresponding to August 11, 3114 BCE. The Long Count allowed the reading of dates recorded on the stelae of ancient Mayan cities, providing a precise understanding of the passage of time in their civilization.

Furthermore, Förstemann made a significant revelation: Mayan symbols should be read from top to bottom rather than from left to right. This crucial observation opened new doors in interpreting the texts and allowed for a more accurate understanding of the rich culture and mathematical knowledge of the Mayans.

However, the discovery of the Long Count led Förstemann to a crossroads. He knew that this would generate controversy and speculation about a supposed "end-of-the-world date." The Long Count concluded on December 21, 2012 AD, marking the end of a Mayan time cycle.

Förstemann understood that, for the Mayans, everything was cyclical, and this date might represent the beginning of a new era rather than a catastrophic event. However, the possibility of a significant event looming ahead raised concerns in his mind and in the minds of those who knew his findings.

Were they facing a warning of a transcendent event for the world?

Uncertainty and anticipation began to envelop Förstemann and those interested in Mayan mysteries. As he continued his research, he debated within himself the multiple interpretations that could arise from the designated date.

The entire world awaited with a mix of fear and hope on December 21, 2012. Would it be an abrupt end or the dawn of a new era for humanity? Only time would reveal the true nature of this mysterious date, hidden in the confines of the Dresden Codex and waiting to be unveiled by those daring to decipher it.

The Long Count was used to record important historical events and to prophesy the distant future. Most fascinating, in addition to its precision, were the different groupings of years, some extremely vast by today's standards. Just as the Gregorian calendar counts series of years known as lustres, decades, centuries, and millennia, the "Long Count" counted series of twenty years, each called Katuns, series of 400 years called Baktuns, series of Long Counts grouping 5200 years, and the famous Hunab-ku, equivalent to 25,625 years. But its calculation didn't end there; they had series grouping 520,000 years, 10.4 million years, and even 208 million years, like the Alautun, something that has scientists puzzled today as the oldest known civilization to date, Sumeria, doesn't surpass 7,500 years. Could it be that the Maya are the product of modern civilizations that have gone extinct several times?

1 kin = 1 day

1 Uinal = 20 kin

1 tun = 360 days = 18 Uinals

1 Katun = 20 tuns = 20 years = 7200 days

1 Baktun = 20 Katuns = 400 years = 144,000 days

1 Long Count = 13 Baktuns = 260 Katuns = 5200 years of 360 days or 5128.76 years of 365 days

5 Long Counts = 1 cycle called Hunab-ku = 25,625 years = 1 Galactic day, "time it takes the sun to complete a cycle around the Galaxy according to Maya culture."

The Maya had, in addition to the Long Count, units representing extremely large values, such as the following:

□	NUM. MAYA	FACTORES QUE MULTIPLICAN	CANTIDAD días/Kines	AÑOS MAYAS	AÑOS GREGORIANOS
Alautun	1	18 20 20 20 13 5 20 20 20	74,880,000,000	208,000,000	205,010,266.9
Kinchiltun	1	18 20 20 20 13 5 20 20 1	3,744,000,000	10,400,000	10,251,608
Kalabtun	1	18 20 20 20 13 5 20 1 1	187,200,000	520,000	512,525.6
Piktun	1	18 20 20 20 13 5 1 1 1	9,360,000	26,000	25,626
Cuentas Largas	1	18 20 20 20 13 1 1 1 1	1,872,000	5,200	5,128
Baktunes	1	18 20 20 20 1 1 1 1 1	144,000	400	394.2
Katunes	1	18 20 20 1 1 1 1 1 1	7,200	200	19.7
Tunes	1	18 20 1 1 1 1 1 1 1	360	1	0.98
Uinales	1	20 1 1 1 1 1 1 1 1	20	0.06	0
Kines	1	1 1 1 1 1 1 1 1 1	1	0.00	0

CHAPTER: THE REVELATION OF THE MAYA GLYPHS

With the meticulously organized Maya corpus and the ongoing interpretation of glyphs, scientists embarked on the exciting task of deciphering the ancient Maya script. They knew that within those mysterious characters lay the key to unveiling the knowledge and history of this enigmatic civilization.

Amidst this quest for knowledge, an exceptional linguist emerged: Yuri Valentinovich Knorosov. Born in the former Soviet Union, in Ukraine, Knorosov became a key figure in the study of Maya writing. Through years of dedication and exhaustive study, he made a discovery that would mark a milestone in understanding Maya glyphs.

Knorosov revealed that the Maya writing system consisted of more than 800 glyphs, functioning as a complex syllabary. Some of these glyphs represented complete words, while others corresponded to specific sounds. The linguist unraveled the syllabary's structure and began assigning sounds and meanings to each glyph, thereby opening a door to the ancient language.

Simultaneously, in another corner of the world, a Russian architect named Tatiana Proskuriakof delved into expeditions to the ruins of Piedras Negras and Yaxchilán. Armed with her passion for drawing and architectural knowledge, Proskuriakof undertook the task of studying Maya stelae and their intricate reliefs.

It was during these explorations that Tatiana made a fascinating discovery: all the stelae recorded detailed biographical aspects of the kings who ruled in those ancient cities. Every carving and inscription told stories of power, conquests, and legacies. Proskuriakof, with her unique ability for drawing and interpreting these reliefs, managed to unveil the living history hidden in the ancient stones.

The findings of Knorosov and Proskuriakof triggered a revolution in the study of Maya writing. Their discoveries quickly spread among the scientific community, ushering in a new era of knowledge and understanding of this ancient civilization.

While the glyphs revealed their secrets and the Maya stelae recounted the stories of past kings, the world marveled at the grandeur and sophistication of Maya culture. Scientists, with a mixture of excitement and humility, delved further into the labyrinths of Maya writing, eager to discover more knowledge and unveil the hidden truths lurking in the depths of the hieroglyphs.

The legacy of the Maya came to life once again, resurfacing from the pages of time and revealing itself as one of the great civilizations of humanity.

CHAPTER 21: THE LEGACY OF SMALL-STONE

The warm and humid air enveloped the small village of Tinún in southeastern Mexico. It was the year 1867, a time when the echoes of the greatness of the Maya still lingered in the collective memory. In this remote corner, Petronila was born into a Maya family, endowed with an exceptional gift and an enormous aptitude for learning the Maya language and its writing.

From her childhood, Petronila showed innate curiosity and skill in the Maya language, particularly in mathematics. With astonishing ease, she learned the arithmetic methods and techniques of her Maya ancestors. Numbers, operations, and calculations became her passion. Aware of her gift, her parents named her "Petronila," which in Maya means "small stone," in honor of her prodigious ability to unravel numerical secrets and read the Maya inscriptions of the Temple of Chichen Itza. She frequently visited the site on weekends to earn some pesos as a guide in the archaeological area.

As she grew, Petronila delighted in applying Maya methods in her mind to solve complex calculations. She challenged friends and family to perform two-digit multiplications, leaving them astonished with her speed and precision. Multiplying 31 by 39, 74 by 76, 62 by 68, or 83 by 87 took her only a few seconds for each operation, leaving those who challenged her speechless.

In her adolescence, inspired by her love for mathematics and the desire to share her knowledge, Petronila decided to adapt Maya calculation methods to the decimal metric system taught in modern schools. It was a way to honor her ancestors while facilitating learning for future generations.

Over time, Petronila became a mother and passed on her mathematical knowledge and the Maya language to her children, and they, in turn, to her grandchildren, who learned, albeit not with as much devotion as she did. However, she remained anonymous for many years until a twist of fate led her to Palenque, home to the majestic Maya ruins.

In 1953, Petronila's son, Manuel, was on vacation in Tortuguero, Palenque. While wandering through the ruins, a group of archaeologists was busy deciphering the enigmatic glyphs of what they called Stela 6. His curiosity and innate knowledge prompted him to approach and observe the stone.

Surprised by the appearance of the young Maya, the archaeologists asked him to step back and let them work, but he was fascinated by the stela. When the archaeologists asked who he was and if he understood Maya glyphs in his ancestral language, he replied, "Le paal chan tuunich," which means "I am the son of small stone." The archaeologists' eyes reflected astonishment upon hearing his response; all southeastern archaeologists had heard of Petronila and her extensive knowledge of Maya culture in Chichen Itza.

As the son of Petronila, Manuel had learned the ancient Maya language since childhood and was equally skilled in reading Maya glyphs. Thus, as he observed the stela in detail, his eyes widened, and what he said left the experts speechless. With a trembling and nervous voice, he told them: "The sacred stela is not complete; it lacks a part, but it warns of something bad that will happen in a few years." The chief archaeologist, astonished by the young man's words, asked him to continue and to translate what the stela said.

Young Manuel replied, "The sacred stela says, 'The thirteenth Baktun will end on 4 Ajaw 3 Kankin, and on that day, Bolon Yokte (God of War) will descend.'" Manuel added, "I recommend converting the long count date to the Gregorian calendar, and you will know when it will happen because, for the Maya, the arrival of Bolon Yokte signifies the end of the Maya world. But beware of the interpretation; there is a blurry part of the stela, and there is also a missing piece, where usually, the event that caused or will cause it is described, and it is not here. So, you will have to look for the missing part to understand why the end of the Maya world is imminent."

The archaeologists, horrified, looked at each other, confirming what they were hearing made sense according to their Maya studies. Now, they held an important part of the Maya prophecy that caused much concern. They concentrated their efforts on searching for the missing piece of the sacred stela but failed to find it. Centuries earlier, it had been discovered and removed from the site by rebellious tribes.

What the archaeologists were unaware of was that the Maya priests, aware of the importance of warning the future Maya generations in time but not sooner, as they wouldn't have all the scientific knowledge to stop it, had chosen the end of the 13th Baktun as the alert date. For the Maya culture, this represents the end of a long count, 5200 Maya years, but at the same time, the beginning of a new era. Thus, the future Maya had 17 tunes (approximately 17 years) to find a way to prevent the collision of asteroids with the planet, enough time if there was scientific progress.

58 years passed, and the discovery of Stela 6 was forgotten until the year 2011 when some archaeologists in Palenque, dusting off museum relics, paused before Stela 6 and published the Maya prophecy. It was then that, as usual, cinemas, books, and media made the most of the misinterpreted catastrophic event by archaeologists. Still, it was well-used by entrepreneurs and hoteliers to make substantial profits from the supposed end of the world on December 21, 2012. After this date passed without any apocalyptic event, people confirmed that the world continued, and everything returned to normal.

While the community wondered what would cause the end of the world, the Itza's Lodge never stopped searching for the second monolith that formed the stela because they knew it held clues to solve the Maya puzzle, despite the reluctance of countries to allow access to the royal codices.

December 21, 2012 side visible to tourists

December 21, 2012 back side

CHAPTER 22: THE SEARCH FOR THE SACRED STELE

The year is 2021, and an aura of mystery and anticipation surrounds the Itza's Lodge. Since time immemorial, they had sought access to the coveted Maya Codices, but these were scattered across three different countries, and their access had been restricted for decades.

The Lodge, aware of the importance of protecting their heritage, remained in a constant state of vigilance. They had received information about an ambitious project called the "Tren Maya," which would bring numerous excavations to the sacred Maya land. It was in this context that the guardians of the past kept their attention alert, ready for any discoveries that might arise during the excavations.

However, their hopes were focused on a particular object: the second monolith of the Sacred Stela. The Lodge knew that this ancient relic held valuable information, a treasure trove of ancestral knowledge that could unveil secrets lost for centuries. Therefore, with a profound sense of responsibility, they had undertaken the task of protecting and safeguarding it.

As time passed, the Lodge had continued searching for clues about the whereabouts of the other half of the Sacred Stela. Connecting scattered threads and following rumors, they became aware of the plans of the Tren Maya and the excavations that would take place in the area. They knew that, amid those development projects, there was the possibility of discovering something transcendental.

CHAPTER 23: THE ENIGMA DISCOVERED

It is August 2021, and as the construction of the famous Tren Maya progresses in the jungle despite heavy rains, a dedicated worker involved in the excavations makes a discovery that will change the course of history. Amidst the thickness of the jungle, covered by a thin layer of mud, he finds an engraved monolith: it is the missing part of Stela 6 found in Tortuguero Palenque and sought by the priests of Pakal. Without fully comprehending the importance of his find, the worker informs the chief of archaeological remains, who immediately halts the work and calls in a team of archaeologists to investigate the newly discovered piece, confirming the discovery: "Chief, it seems to be the missing part of the sacred stela found in Palenque," responds one of the researchers, leaving the Chief Archaeologist stunned by the enormous discovery.

The news of the mysterious discovery spreads rapidly, and both the archaeological community and the members of the Itza's Lodge are on edge. The sacred stela, composed of two monoliths and hidden for centuries in the dense jungle, seems poised to reveal its deepest secrets.

As archaeologists carefully examine the now complete sacred stela, more questions than answers arise. The glyphs carved into the ancient stone are an enigma, a coded message waiting to be deciphered.

The chief of archaeological remains, aware of the importance of this discovery, quickly contacts the grand master of the Itza's Lodge. The news circulates as a whisper among the lodge members, who are both captivated and concerned about what this discovery might unleash.

The most experienced archaeologists find themselves at a crucial point in the plot, facing the task of deciphering the secrets that the sacred stela conceals. Among them are linguists specializing in Maya writing, historians, and archaeologists passionate about ancestral history. Together, they immerse themselves in the ancient wisdom and knowledge of the Maya, searching for clues and connections that will guide them to the hidden truth behind the carved glyphs, even attempting to decipher some of the blurry glyphs.

Every detail, every inscription on the sacred stela, could reveal a secret that will alter the understanding of Maya history and its connection to the future. Meanwhile, the construction work of the Tren Maya temporarily halts; the area is immediately cordoned off and protected from the elements. The discovered enigma becomes the center of attention, and all eyes turn towards this piece of history that has emerged from the depths of the jungle.

CHAPTER 24: THE HEAVENLY SECRETS

Aware of the astronomical significance of the discovered sacred stela, the members of the Itza's Lodge secretly meet with the chief archaeologist of the area to request permission for the study and documentation of the sacred stela without arousing suspicions.

The grand master of the Lodge, with his keen and perceptive gaze, realizes that the glyphs engraved on the second monolith correspond to astronomical positions indicated in the Royal Codices. Aware of the need for an expert in the field, he decides to hire an astronomer with extensive experience, but of Maya origin, to avoid raising suspicions within the scientific community.

This is how Selena, a woman with vast experience dedicated to research at the prestigious Institute of Astronomy at UNAM, becomes a crucial part of deciphering King Pakal's omen. Selena, besides being a renowned astronomer, has Maya roots that trace back to her great-grandmother Petronila, born in Tinún in the Municipality of Campeche, who spent her vacations in Chichen Itza with her great-grandmother year after year since childhood. Her knowledge and connection to ancient Maya culture make her the perfect candidate to unravel the celestial secrets enclosed in the sacred stela.

Under the veil of mystery and with caution, the Itza's Lodge introduces Selena into their circle of trust. With an inquisitive mind and respect for her cultural heritage, Selena immerses herself in the study of the astronomical glyphs engraved on the sacred stela. Every stroke, every symbol, reveals an ancestral story and profound knowledge of the stars.

Alongside the members of the Lodge, Selena discovers that the ancient Maya possessed extraordinary wisdom regarding celestial phenomena. The glyphs represent stellar alignments, planetary movements, and astronomically significant events. The sacred stela seems to indicate that there is a coded map of the apocalyptic event in the Royal Codices, a detailed legacy left by the ancient Maya to guide future generations and solve the enigma.

As Selena delves deeper into her research, she immerses herself in a fascinating world where the past and present intertwine. Through ancestral wisdom and scientific knowledge, she untangles the threads of the cosmos woven into the glyphs engraved on the sacred stela. Each discovery is a step closer to understanding the ancient Maya and their profound connection with the universe.

CHAPTER 25: THE COSMIC ENIGMS

Selena, after carefully examining the stela, realizes that an apocalyptic astronomical event has been recorded. However, the message refers to the Royal Codices, prompting her to consider where to find the answer to the enigma enclosed in the sacred stela.

Selena knows that to pinpoint the location of a planet in the solar system or any celestial object, two sets of coordinates are generally used: equatorial coordinates and ecliptic coordinates.

Equatorial coordinates are based on the projection of Earth's coordinate system onto the sky. The primary coordinate is right ascension (RA), similar to terrestrial longitude, measured in hours, minutes, and seconds. The other coordinate is declination (Dec), analogous to terrestrial latitude, measured in degrees, minutes, and seconds. Together, right ascension and declination provide the precise location of a celestial object in relation to Earth.

Ecliptic coordinates are based on the plane of the ecliptic, which is the orbital plane of Earth around the Sun. The primary coordinate is ecliptic longitude (λ), measuring the angular position of the planet along the ecliptic and expressed in degrees. The other coordinate is ecliptic latitude (β), measuring the deviation of the planet from the ecliptic plane, also expressed in degrees.

Aware of the need for more information to decipher the enigma, Selena and the grand Master understand that one of the three Codices must have been chosen by the Mayan priests to house the vast set of astronomical coordinates for all celestial references, thus enabling the precise determination of a cosmic event's location in the future.

The grand Master of the Itza's Lodge tells Selena, "I believe I know which one, that Codex must be the Dresden Codex; only it, given its enormous extent, could accommodate all the astronomical coordinates in the Mayan language necessary to unravel the cosmic position hidden in the sacred stela."

The grand master of the Itza's Lodge explains to Selena, "The Codex is a manuscript on folded papyrus accordion-style and must have at least 39 pages, although some sections are damaged or missing; it has a total length of approximately 3.56 meters when fully unfolded, with each page being about 20 centimeters in height and variable in length, as some pages are longer than others."

Once again, Selena is amazed by the wisdom of the Itza's Lodge and agrees with the grand Master to embark on a journey to the old continent in search of forgotten knowledge and ancient mysteries safeguarded in a foreign but interesting and cultured country.

Despite travel restrictions due to the pandemic of an acute respiratory virus called SARS-II, Selena travels in September of 2021 to Dresden, Germany, a place full of history and knowledge. There, she meets experts on the Codex, which has survived over time since its transfer to Madrid by Hernán Cortés and later to Germany, where it was extracted from its place of safeguarding and stolen as part of the war booty by the Nazis in World War II. The Codex reveals itself as an invaluable source of wisdom, preserving the secrets and prophecies of the ancient Maya.

Selena, driven by her passion and curiosity and after numerous obstacles to obtain permits, manages to access the Codex and immerses herself in the fascinating study. Each page unfolded before her is like opening a door to a universe lost in time. The Maya symbols and glyphs come to life under her attentive gaze, revealing clues and precise astronomical positions of celestial bodies that could shed light on the enigma of the sacred stela.

As Selena delves into the depths of the Dresden Codex, she discovers that the prophecy engraved on the sacred stela is only a part of a complex web of Mayan knowledge. The ancient Mayan astronomers had foreseen significant cosmic events and had accurately recorded them in their Codices. The revelation of the end of the Maya world was just a date to pinpoint in a larger puzzle, a couple of pieces that Selena is determined to unravel.

In an atmosphere of mystery and anticipation, as Selena immerses herself in the Dresden Codex in search of answers, each stroke becomes a step closer to the hidden truth in the Maya mysteries. Through her determination and knowledge, Selena becomes a link between the past and the present, between the ancient Mayan sages and the omen of their king to alert modern humanity.

CHAPTER 26: THE ENIGMA UNVEILED

While the mystery of the sacred stele remains shrouded in shadows, a new figure emerges in the quest. The head archaeologist, intrigued by the mysterious visit of the grand master of the Itza's, decides to take matters into his own hands and seek answers. Aware of the importance of the discovery, he decides to enlist the help of Emmanuel, an architect specializing in religious relics and antiquities, to unravel the enigma surrounding the stele.

Imbued with the magnitude of the challenge before him, Emmanuel delves into a meticulous analysis of the piece of the sacred stele. Every inscription, every detail carved into the ancient stone, is examined with precision and patience. After long hours of study and reflection, Emmanuel arrives at two conclusions that resonate with the Chief Archaeologist. The part of the stele found corresponds to the missing part of Stele 6 discovered in Tortuguero, Palenque, which references the end of the Mayan world. The second conclusion suggests that the event is detailed in the Royal Codices, making it essential to travel to Madrid and consult the Codex housed in the National Library of Spain, as it is, to his knowledge, the best-preserved and language would not pose an issue.

The chief archaeologist, aware of the potential this new stage of research holds, does not hesitate to consult with his superiors at the Institute of Anthropology and History. After careful deliberation, they secure the necessary permissions in Spain and grant Emmanuel authorization to travel to Madrid and immerse himself in the sea of ancient Mayan knowledge guarded in Europe.

Emmanuel immediately embarks on a journey filled with mysteries, chasing the traces left by the wise Mayans in the past. Madrid becomes a pivotal destination for him, where the long-awaited answers and keys that could unveil the mystery of the sacred stele are housed.

Emmanuel arrives at Barajas Airport in Madrid in September 2021, aware that each step brings him closer to the truth hidden in the symbols carved into the sacred stele and to a great mystery on the verge of discovery. He knows he must be cautious with the curators guarding the Codex in the Library, as they might deny him access if they suspect the reason behind his interest.

As Emmanuel approaches Madrid, the secrets of the Mayan past seem to come to life, waiting to be unveiled in the pages of the ancient Codex. The doors to a complete understanding of the puzzle are about to open, and Emmanuel's fate becomes a thread that connects the past and present in an unwavering quest for lost knowledge.

CHAPTER 27: CELESTIAL REVELATIONS

The intense quest to unravel the mystery has diverged into two distinct paths, yet both seeking the same answer. While Emmanuel is investigating the Codex in Madrid, Selena delves into the National Library of Dresden, eager to unveil the secrets locked within the ancient Codex. Both pursue the truth with determination, each with their own objective and destiny in mind.

Surrounded by books referencing the 800 Maya glyphs and their meanings, Selena immerses herself in ancestral knowledge, feeling the excitement and responsibility of her task. Within the pages of the Maya Codex, she discovers two crucial dates that resonate with the fate of the ancient civilization.

The first astronomical event marked in time, the asteroid fall on August 28, 683 b.c. emerges in her research and cosmic catastrophe that left its mark on the annals of Maya history, narrated in the Codex as the serpent descending from the sky to end the Maya world, prompting them to evacuate to Palenque following King Pakal.

But the most astonishing revelation comes when Selena realizes that the Dresden Real Codex describes the precise astronomical coordinates of the planets Mars, Venus, Jupiter, Saturn, and the two asteroids on the day of the cosmic phenomenon, 1346 years later. Amazed by the astronomical data provided by the nearly 39 pages of the Codex, she begins to take photographs of each one thanks to a hidden camera she cleverly carried among her clothes.

With the need for more answers, Selena wastes no time and immediately communicates with the grand master of the Itza's. Selena explains the major discovery and requests authorization to travel to France and consult the Paris Codex, housed in the prestigious Louvre Museum in France, which could reveal a crucial piece of information: the date of the impending catastrophic cosmic event. Some pages are damaged, requiring deciphering the enigma surrounding the Maya omen.

The grand master of the Itza's gives his approval and sends funds for Selena to travel to France immediately. Upon her arrival, Selena strolls through the Parisian streets, feeling the weight of history and time on her shoulders. She finds herself drawn into the intensity of the journey and, unable to share her concern with a third party, decides to have a coffee and try a blackberry pastry, her favorite, in front of the Champs-Élysées as the opening time of the Louvre Museum approaches, where the second Codex holds the long-awaited answers.

While Selena and Emmanuel venture into solving the Maya mystery, their minds immerse in a universe of prophecies and cosmic catastrophes. Every step of Selena and Emmanuel brings them closer to the truth hidden in the sacred texts of the Maya, and destiny seems to conspire to reveal the deepest secrets they can imagine.

CHAPTER 28: THE SECRETS OF THE WORN CODEX

While Selena has arrived in Paris, Emmanuel, filled with anticipation, immerses himself in the reading of the Codex lying before him. Among the worn pages, he manages to discover a crucial clue: the exact location where the first asteroid landed in Maya territory. Eighty kilometers off the coast of Kankun, a place that evokes both natural beauty and imminent danger.

But the most surprising revelation is reserved for him as he deciphers in the Codex the cause: a second and third asteroid are destined to impact directly on Chichen Itza. The magnitude of this prediction awakens a deep unease in Emmanuel's heart. However, his progress is halted by the deterioration of the Codex, as the date of the event is displayed incompletely.

With the urgency to find the date of the apocalyptic event, Emmanuel does not hesitate to contact the head archaeologist. With sincere fear and determination, he shares the need to travel to Paris to investigate the Maya Codex housed in the Louvre Museum. There, he hopes to find the missing date and details of the puzzle that will reveal the Maya omen to the world.

The head archaeologist, aware of the historical significance of the sacred stele they had discovered, did not hesitate for a moment to approve Emmanuel's trip to Paris. He knew that the young researcher had the ability and passion necessary to carry out the mission successfully.

Without wasting time, the head archaeologist went to his office and, with a mix of anticipation and concern, managed the permits through government offices and provided the necessary funds for Emmanuel to fly to the City of Lights as soon as possible. He knew that time was a crucial factor, and every minute counted in this exciting quest for answers.

However, before Emmanuel departed, the head archaeologist called him into his office for a serious and momentous conversation. He warned him with a serious and firm tone that he must keep the true reasons for his trip absolutely secret. He explained that disclosing the importance of the sacred stele research could trigger collective hysteria, both in academic circles and in society at large.

The head archaeologist emphasized the need to protect the integrity of the discovery and to avoid any interference that could hinder their work. Only a few trusted individuals were aware of the true magnitude of the sacred stele, and it was imperative to keep it a secret until all the necessary data had been collected.

Firmly, the head archaeologist urged Emmanuel to be discreet and cautious in his interactions in Paris. He reminded him that he was representing the entire team of archaeologists and that his behavior and words should reflect the seriousness and professionalism.

After giving him these instructions, the head archaeologist shook Emmanuel's hand sincerely and wished him good luck on his journey. Thus, with a crucial mission and the weight of an ancestral secret on his shoulders, Emmanuel arrived promptly in Paris, determined to decipher the mysteries surrounding the sacred stele and protect it from any danger that might arise from revealing its true significance, unaware that Selena would also be enjoying a delicious coffee nearby.

CHAPTER 29: THE MEETING AT THE MUSEUM

Both Selena and Emmanuel have arrived in the majestic city of Paris separately. Both have followed the call of history and the Mayan Codices, without suspecting that their destiny would lead them to cross paths in the iconic Louvre Museum, which houses the Codex taken as war loot by Napoleon during his invasion of Europe.

With surprising synchronicity, Selena and Emmanuel find themselves in the same room where the ancient document is safeguarded. When they request access to the Codex from the curator, they turn to each other with eyes of astonishment, realizing the strange coincidence. They immediately lock eyes, intrigued by the connection that binds them, trying to scrutinize the interest in the same archaeological piece.

A friendly conversation initiated by Emmanuel breaks the ice between them: "From what I've seen and heard, you're a Mexican scientist, right?" to which Selena responds with a smile, "If my lab coat gives me away, but it seems you're an architect from UNAM, am I wrong? Haha," Emmanuel smiles, realizing he was wearing the classic blue and gold university jacket.

The conversation unfolds pleasantly between them, revealing notable similarities in their background, nationality, and academic training. Destiny has conspired to unite these two researchers in their common quest across the Atlantic.

Amidst the grandeur of the artworks surrounding them, Selena and Emmanuel share their individual discoveries about the Mayan Codices. Excited and filled with awe, they disclose the data they have managed to decipher so far. Both have found the date of the first asteroid that threatened the Mayan world: the first, an event that occurred in the year 680 AD. However, they quickly find in the Royal Codex of Paris the date of the second apocalyptic event, set as 13.0.16.15.6 in Chichen Itza as their ultimate goal. Nevertheless, the mystery persists: what role does the smaller asteroid, apparently less significant but equally crucial, play? They both realize that only by working together can they unveil the last secret held by the smaller asteroid.

CHAPTER 30: THE COSMIC REVELATION

Selena and Emmanuel immerse themselves in the reading of the Mayan Codex safeguarded in Paris. In their hands, they hold a crucial testimony of the disappearance of the ancient Maya culture, and now they are on the verge of unraveling secrets that have remained hidden for centuries.

With each deciphered line, the observers of the past discover the ominous fate looming over Chichen Itza and possibly the entire world. The images recorded in the Codex also reveal the apocalyptic event in which the sea would devour the majestic pyramid of Chichen Itza, leading to the disappearance of the great Maya civilization due to the impact of a large asteroid.

On the other hand, the confirmation of the arrival of two imminent asteroids adds an element of horror to the revelation. The studies conducted by Selena and Emmanuel allow them to understand that one of the asteroids, similar in size to the one that destroyed the reign of the great Pakal, is on a collision course with Earth. The second celestial rock, though small in size, is also on its way, triggering additional fears.

With their minds immersed in the vast knowledge of the Maya and their profound connections with the cosmos, Selena and Emmanuel were absorbed in the reading of the ancient Codices. These treasures of ancestral wisdom revealed secrets that resonated deep within their beings. With each page they turned, valuable data about the asteroids unfolded before their eyes, providing them with a clearer understanding of the magnitude of the impending danger.

Selena, with her bright eyes and agile mind, connected the dots and deciphered the hidden messages in the Codices. The stars seemed to whisper their most intimate secrets to her, revealing the trajectories of the asteroids with astonishing precision. Emmanuel, on his part, admired the ingenuity and brilliance of the ancient Maya, who had anticipated and recorded these celestial events long before modern humanity was aware of their existence.

However, as the truth materialized before them, a storm of conflicting emotions swept through their hearts. Wonder and admiration for the Maya legacy mixed with the overwhelming responsibility to warn humanity about the imminent threat. They knew they possessed information that could change the course of history, but they also feared the reaction that this news could trigger.

Faced with the crossroads between the duty to protect humanity and the fear of collective hysteria, Selena and Emmanuel weighed every word and action. They knew they had to act with caution and wisdom, balancing the need to share information with the need to preserve social stability. The responsibility resting on their shoulders was overwhelming, but their commitment to the well-being of humanity surpassed any fear.

Aware of the importance of their mission, Selena and Emmanuel prepared to face the challenges ahead. Together, armed with ancestral knowledge and unwavering determination, they embarked on a journey that transcended time and space. Their goal was clear: to warn humanity about the imminent danger and find a solution to preserve the future of Earth.

Amidst uncertainty and fear, Selena and Emmanuel would become beacons of hope and guidance for those willing to listen. Their mission was not only scientific but also a call to unity and human collaboration in a critical moment. Together, they would face the challenge with courage, never losing sight of the legacy of the Maya and their vision of a future in harmony with the cosmos.

Thus, with the weight of ancestral knowledge and the responsibility to warn humanity, Selena and Emmanuel ventured into a world of mystery and danger, guided by the wisdom of the ancient Maya and their commitment to a better future.

CHAPTER 31: THE ENIGMA OF ASTEROIDS

Selena, with her vast astronomical experience, delves into the search for answers in the databases of the prestigious Institute of Astronomy at UNAM. The puzzle tormenting her is the discrepancy between the Mayan prophecies and contemporary astronomical data.

With skill and meticulousness, Selena discovers with the help of the Stelarium application and the Sentry System (highly automated collision monitoring system) that, given the astronomical positions of the planets mentioned in the Codices, the two asteroids mentioned in the sacred stele are none other than Apophis and 2012 XE133.

Apophis, an asteroid with a diameter of 314 meters that has approached Earth several times, and according to astronomical system data, could dangerously approach Earth, but not until 2068. This will happen relatively closely in 2029, along with 2012 XE133, a smaller asteroid but with no possibility of collision. A perplexing contradiction arises for Selena: NAS@ calculations and scientific data indicate that both asteroids will only pass near our planet without absolute collision with Earth, dismissing any possible impact. However, the Maya data speak of a collision.

According to NAS@, 2012 XE133 is an Aten asteroid, meaning it is a temporary co-orbital asteroid of Venus. It has a diameter of 72 meters and is considered a potentially hazardous object since it periodically comes within 0.05 AU of Earth. Its next approach to Earth will be on December 30, 2028.

This discrepancy raises questions in Selena's mind. She wonders, how could the Maya foresee a collision with Earth, while modern astronomical studies and current systems do not corroborate that event? The astronomer faces a bewildering dilemma: how to reconcile Maya precision with contemporary data? Is it possible that the Maya made an error in their calculations? Is it possible that there is something deeper and more mysterious that they discovered, and we are yet to unveil despite our advancements?

As the mystery intensifies, Selena plunges into a frenzied search for additional clues in the Codices, deepening her knowledge and contacts in the scientific community. Her findings could unveil the key to understanding the Maya prophecy and the true nature of the impending danger.

The fate of the world is at stake. Selena embarks on a race against time to unravel the hidden truth behind astronomical data and Maya prophecies. The tension rises as she struggles to discover the connection between imminent cosmic events and the ancient knowledge of the early Maya, which was virtually erased since the first sun with the fall of the Chicxulub asteroid, which impacted the Yucatan Peninsula and led to the extinction of dinosaurs 66 million years ago.

It happened in spring, in the first sun, amid the splendor of a day of sprouts and newcomers from Orion in the ship of Kukulkan, populating the northern hemisphere of the Earth when they would receive a lethal blow to their biosphere. The impact of Chicxulub was so great that about 75% of the plant and animal species existing on the planet became extinct. With an approximate diameter of 14 kilometers, Chicxulub changed the natural course of life on the Earth's surface forever, ending the reign of dinosaurs and all forms of life, only saved by those who returned to Orion.

Chicxulub translates from Maya as the 'tail of the Devil.' After the impact, Chicxulub left a massive crater 180 kilometers wide and 900 meters deep on the Yucatan Peninsula, south of Mexico, visible only from space. The most incredible thing is that nothing has been preserved from this cosmic rock. This crater eluded scientists' technology for decades, being perfectly hidden beneath local sediment and rocks.

For a year after the impact, perpetual night flooded the Earth's skies. Due to a heavy ash cloud, sunlight did not reach the surface for months, temperatures dropped below 0°C, and species inhabiting the planet could not adapt. Thus ended the era of dinosaurs at the conclusion of the sixth Kinchiltun (one Kinchiltun = 10,251,608 years).

CHAPTER 32: SUMERKED TREASURES

November 2021 unfolds as Selena and Emmanuel return to their beloved land, Mexico, determined to explore the impact zone of the potential asteroid foretold by the Mayan priests, which fell into the waters of Yucatán on March 21, 650 AD.

With the purpose of unraveling the secrets hidden beneath the ocean floor, they find themselves in Puerto Progreso with a group of expert divers hired by a company to conduct underwater explorations in the area. After sharing the prophecy of King Pakal with them, they decide to invite them to a zone where they have observed ancient remnants of a civilization closely related to the Mayan culture.

For the Canadian oceanographer named Paulina, the lead scientist in the discovery in 2011, these structures were a mystery she had set out to solve after associating them with the ruins found in the archaeological site of Dzibilchaltún, located northwest of Yucatán. Selena and Emmanuel's expertise in Mayan culture were of great value to her.

Filled with enthusiasm and adrenaline, and after 18 hours sailing into the sea towards Cuba and departing from Puerto Progreso, the sonar indicates a series of structures at a depth of 660 meters. It is then that they dive into the crystal-clear waters with the help of a submersible, and as they descend into the ocean depths, Selena and Emmanuel's hearts beat rapidly, aware that they are about to encounter an archaeological treasure hidden for centuries that could change the history of Mayan culture.

As the submersible dives deeper, the mystery intensifies. After 30 minutes of searching and being only 8 kilometers from Cabo San Antonio, Cuba, the vehicle's lights illuminating the dark ocean reveal an astonishing sight: a gigantic and beautiful archaeological site emerges before their eyes, a treasure hidden beneath the waves, the remains of the Mother Island, three ancestral pyramids in a vast archaeological area.

To their own surprise, the submerged ruins extend like a forgotten legacy, displaying their majesty and splendor in the depths of the sea. The ancient structures, temples, and lost treasures seem to whisper stories of an ancestral civilization that once thrived there.

For Paulina and her team, the constructions date back to 10 to 12,000 years old, but they are unaware of how long they have been submerged. Selena and Emmanuel, extremely excited and amazed by Paulina's magnificent discovery, delve into the submerged ruins, exploring every corner with reverence and respect. Each discovery reveals answers to their questions and challenges their previous archaeological knowledge.

For Selena and Emmanuel, everything now becomes clear: the fall of the great meteor that destroyed the Yucatán Peninsula, forewarned by Pakal, was the consequence of an advanced Mayan civilization that predates Pakal disappearing overnight. Their mathematical and astronomical advancements were buried beneath the waves, at the bottom of the sea. The colossal impact off the peninsula resulted in a massive tsunami that abruptly wiped out the Mayan people, leaving only their visible testimony on the side of the Chichen Itza pyramid.

As they swim among the ruins, Selena and Emmanuel immerse themselves in a world of mysteries and possibilities. Each object found whispers lost stories, and the exodus that the Mayans had to face as they fled to Palenque for survival drives them to continue exploring. They are aware that this discovery has the potential to change the understanding of the entire Mayan history and to reveal hidden truths that could answer the questions posed for centuries by the Mayans and various earlier civilizations.

CHAPTER 33: MAYAN WISDOM

Selena and Emmanuel, filled with astonishment at the discovery of the submerged ruins, decide to meet in Tulum to carefully analyze the data collected from the Codices and decipher the pending enigma. Aware of the discrepancy between the Mayan prophecy and contemporary astronomical calculations, they gather with determination to unravel the mystery that could change the planet's destiny.

As Selena examines the Codex closely, a spark of understanding begins to illuminate her mind. The words inscribed on the ancient parchment seem to reveal a surprising truth: the asteroid 2012 XE133 is not destined to collide directly with Earth. Instead, the Mayans are attempting to warn us that its trajectory would intersect with the path of the asteroid Apophis, altering its course and directing it toward Earth, causing a significant impact and the extinction of future Mayans.

The puzzle pieces start to fall into place. If 2012 XE133 diverts Apophis's route, altering its original course, this would mean that the impact date would also be modified. The date found in the Paris Codex, referring to the second asteroid in the long count, is 13.0.16.15.6, corresponding to a day in July 2029 as the collision date. Therefore, modern astronomical calculations indicate that Apophis will be closer to Earth on April 13, 2029, as they haven't considered the collision between them and the change in trajectory and impact dates on Earth.

Selena realizes that, to achieve such precise calculations by the Mayans, they must have accurately calculated the trajectories of the two cosmic objects and their collision 1500 years before the event. She proceeds to review the calculations.

Selena then reviews the calculation algorithms, explaining to Emmanuel how to confirm them. First, says Selena, we must translate the glyphs into the numerical system of the Mayan long count by integrating the visible glyphs referring to the date of the apocalypse from the 3 Codices.

Seeing the glyphs, Selena and Emmanuel confirm that it is the long count referring to 13 Baktun, 0 Katun, 16 Tun, 15 Uinal, 6 Kín, 12 Kimi, 4 Yazkin, Lord of the Night G9.

Then, says Selena, we need to calculate how many Mayan days would have passed since the start of the long count to that date:

13 Baktuns x 144,000 days = 1,872,000 days

0 Katuns = 0 days

16 Tuns x 360 days = 5760 days

15 Uinals x 20 days = 300 days

6 Kin = 6 days

The total number of days that the Mayans indicate would have passed since the start of the long count is a total of 1,878,066 Mayan days.

To calculate the date according to the Gregorian calendar, which is currently in use, it is essential to consider how the Mayans calculated the solar year.

For the Mayans, the approximate duration of the solar year was 365.24 days. This estimation was quite precise and closely approached the currently accepted value.

However, unlike the Gregorian calendar used today, the Mayan calendar did not include a regular leap year system to adjust the discrepancy between the solar year's duration and the length of the calendar year. Instead, the Mayans used a more complex and accurate method to maintain correspondence between their calendar and astronomical cycles.

The Mayan calendar consisted of various cycles, including the Tzolk'in (sacred calendar of 260 days) and the Haab' (solar calendar of 365 days). These two calendars combined into what is known as a "long count," which was a sequence of longer time units.

The annual adjustment was made by adding an additional day at the end of the last month of the Haab', known as Uayeb. This additional month had only five or six days in leap years following the Calendar Round and was considered a transitional and precautionary period. During these five or six days, as appropriate, the Mayans held special ceremonies and avoided certain activities.

To make adjustments and maintain synchronization between their calendar and astronomical events, the Mayans used a cycle called the "Calendar Round." This Calendar Round combined the Tzolk'in and the Haab' in a 52-year cycle. After each 52-year cycle, the Mayans had a mechanism for precise corrections and adjustments.

Through this system of corrections and adjustments, the Mayans managed to maintain precise synchronization between their calendar and astronomical events, allowing them to make almost exact calculations and keep proper track of time in their society.

If we want to calculate the date according to the Gregorian calendar, which is currently in use, we must consider that the year 3114 BCE was not a leap year according to the Julian calendar (every four years), and the year 2029 CE was not a leap year according to the Gregorian calendar. Leap years are those divisible by 4, except for years divisible by 100 but not by 400. Understanding this, we can perform the calculation.

Selena consults the computer at the Institute of Astronomy and asks it to calculate the date if 1,878,066 days have passed, considering leap days. The computer responds that the total number of days according to the Gregorian calendar results in the date of July 31, 2029. Selena can't believe the date; she is almost fainting: it corresponds to the day and month of her father's birthday, also of Mayan origin! He had followed the number 13 throughout his life; he lived in Mexico City in postal zone 13, played American football in his youth with the number 13, died on January 13, and was born on July 31, which is a reverse 13! Extremely moved by the discovery, she decides to manually review the calculations of the Institute of Astronomy's computer:

Calculation of complete years:

From 3114 BCE to 1 BCE = 3113 complete years and fraction.

From 1 CE to 2029 CE = 2028 complete years and fraction.

Calculation of leap years:

From 3114 BCE to 1 BCE, every 4 years has a leap year. Therefore, 3114/4 gives 778 leap years.

From 1 CE to 2029 CE, there are 508 leap years (2029/4).

Calculation of remaining days in incomplete years:

From August 11 to December 31, 3114 BCE, there are 142 days.

From January 1 to July 31, 2029 CE, there are 211 days.

Calculation of the total number of days:

To calculate the total number of days, Selena added the days of complete years, the days of leap years, and the remaining days in the initial and final years:

(3113 complete years x 365 days) + (778 leap years) + (2028 complete years x 365 days) + (508 leap years) + the fractions of the initial and final years, which are 142 + 211 days, resulting in 1,878,065 days, only a one-day difference in almost

CHAPTER 34: THE AWAKENING OF CONSCIENCES

The date marked on the calendar is inexorably approaching, and Selena and Emmanuel know that every minute counts. Physically separated but united by their groundbreaking discovery, they hurry to inform the right people about the imminent threat facing humanity.

Selena, with her heart beating with excitement, heads to the headquarters of the Itza's Lodge. There, in front of the wise elders, she shares all the details of the discovery that will change the course of history. The members of the Lodge, aware of the importance of this revelation, listen attentively as Selena explains the connection between ancient Mayan knowledge and modern astronomical data.

Meanwhile, Emmanuel returns to Yucatán, where the head of archaeology reports the astonishing findings to the President of Mexico, who has arrived to personally oversee the progress of the Mayan train. In the midst of the excitement, Emmanuel approaches the head of archaeology and shares the crucial details of the discovery related to the Mayan enigma and the imminent threat of asteroids.

Aware of the significance of this information, both the director of the Institute of Astronomy of Mexico and the head of archaeology understand the need to take immediate action. The news spreads rapidly, and scientists, archaeologists, and government leaders gather in a joint effort to assess the situation and find a solution.

Society as a whole is caught in a whirlwind of emotions. Uncertainty mixes with hope as the news spreads, and collective awareness rises in the face of the imminent threat hanging over humanity. Everywhere, people begin to realize the fragility of life and the importance of global collaboration to face this cosmic challenge.

The clock continues to advance relentlessly toward the fateful date, and humanity is in a race against time to find a solution and avoid a collision with the asteroids.

CHAPTER 35: THE ALLIANCE IN SEARCH OF THE TRUTH

The rumor of the groundbreaking discovery spreads like wildfire in the wind. The news has reached the ears of the rector of the National Autonomous University of Mexico and the head of archaeology, who recognize the urgency to act and seek the necessary support to validate the finding and face the imminent threat.

With determination and responsibility, the Rector and the head of Archaeology request a meeting with the President of Mexico. They understand that the gravity of the situation requires a joint effort and global collaboration. In this crucial meeting, they present the discovery and call for cooperation with the United States of America.

The request is clear: to seek the support of NASA, the prestigious American space agency, to scientifically validate and support the obtained data. Aware of the importance of this alliance and the magnitude of the challenge they face, the President of Mexico and his advisors understand the need to take immediate action and coordinate efforts with the international scientific community.

Diplomatic efforts are set in motion, and through appropriate channels, a dialogue is established between Mexico and the United States. The UNAM, with its worldwide recognition in the academic and scientific fields, becomes a communication bridge between Mexican experts and NASA.

Amidst uncertainty and time progressing relentlessly, the scientific community and world leaders unite in a joint effort to validate the authenticity of the discovery. The data collected by Selena and Emmanuel undergo rigorous analysis and testing, while NASA experts contribute their expertise and technological resources to verify the existence of the asteroids and assess their trajectories.

The wait is long and tense, but finally, after painstaking work and a thorough joint evaluation, the truth of the discovery is confirmed. The United States of America, aware of the gravity of the situation, commit to collaborating with Mexico and the international community to find solutions and mitigate the danger looming over humanity.

The news of the alliance between Mexico and the United States spreads rapidly, and global awareness unites in a collective effort to face this cosmic challenge.

The sun began to rise on the horizon as Selena and Emmanuel prepared for a transcendent journey to NASA. Full of excitement and determination, they boarded the plane that would take them to the headquarters of the space agency in the United States. Destiny had granted them the responsibility to validate a discovery that could have far-reaching repercussions for humanity.

Upon arriving at NASA facilities, they were welcomed by a group of renowned scientists, specialists in the study of asteroids and their trajectories. The gazes of Selena and Emmanuel met, loaded with determination and a firm purpose in mind: to convince these experts from the National Autonomous University of Mexico that the danger was real and required immediate attention.

CHAPTER 36: THE CULTURAL DEBATE

The scientists at NASA, at first glance, considered that the newly discovered asteroids would pass close to Earth but without posing a direct collision threat. However, Selena and Emmanuel were not willing to accept that conclusion without further scrutiny. With courage and solid foundations supported by their research, they began to present their argument against that view.

A scientific debate unfolded within the NASA facilities. Bright minds clashed, each passionately defending their viewpoint with knowledge and conviction. Selena and Emmanuel presented every detail of their research, emphasizing the possibility that even a slight variation in the asteroids' trajectory could endanger the planet's safety.

The atmosphere became tense and expectant as NASA scientists attentively listened to the arguments of the fearless Mexican researchers and the information unveiled in the Codices. On one side, there were decades of experience and recognition within the space agency; on the other, the enthusiasm and dedication of Selena and Emmanuel to safeguard humanity from a potential catastrophe thanks to the advanced astronomical knowledge of the Mayans.

The debate extended for hours as scientists analyzed data, conducted simulations, and considered all possibilities. Finally, a voice rose in the silence of the room. It was one of the NASA scientists who, after intense data analysis and trajectory simulations of both asteroids, admitted that the asteroid's trajectory could intersect with Apophis days before its approach to Earth, causing it to divert its course and impact the planet on the date calculated by King Pakal and his Mayan priests. Therefore, working with the help of computers to refine this potential catastrophic event was necessary.

Selena and Emmanuel looked at each other with a mixture of relief and satisfaction and embraced. They had succeeded in making an impact on the most renowned scientific community in the world. Their bravery and persistence had been worthwhile.

From that moment on, the scientific group from NASA and the researchers from UNAM worked hand in hand, combining their knowledge and efforts to monitor the trajectory of the asteroids more precisely and assess any changes in their course. Together, they would take preventive measures and develop contingency plans to protect Earth in case of a potential dangerous approach.

Selena and Emmanuel, now recognized and respected by the scientific group, became influential voices to initiate a deep analysis of this hypothesis and determine the necessary action plans to try to avoid the catastrophe.

CHAPTER 37: THE PROGRAMMING OF THE PATHS

Selena and the scientists at NASA gathered in the main laboratory, surrounded by computer screens and an atmosphere filled with tension. It was the crucial moment to refine the trajectories of the asteroids Apophis and, most importantly, the asteroid 2012 XE133, and to determine the day and time of their collision.

With skill and precision, Selena entered the data into the system and programmed the computer to generate the trajectories of both asteroids. The scientists watched attentively as the screen displayed the trajectories of celestial bodies in space.

The silence took hold of the laboratory as everyone awaited the results. Eyes were fixed on the trajectories unfolding before them. Selena and the NASA scientists crossed their fingers, hoping that the evidence would confirm their suspicions and allow them to take the necessary measures to prevent a disaster.

Finally, the simulations were completed, and the results appeared on the main screen. Selena and the NASA scientists held their breath as they analyzed the presented data. According to the trajectories generated by the computer, the asteroids would indeed collide, and Apophis would deviate with a collision course towards Earth.

The theory of the asteroid collision had been confirmed in all computational runs. The news hit the laboratory like a sledgehammer. Time became a precious and urgent resource. Selena and the NASA scientists knew they had to act quickly to avert a catastrophe.

Pooling their experience and knowledge, both groups of scientists joined in an unprecedented collaboration. Together, they crafted a meticulous plan involving a mission with advanced technology and the joint efforts of international space agencies. The main mission was to divert the trajectory of the smaller asteroid and steer it away from the collision path with Apophis to prevent its impact on Earth.

Days and nights blended as scientists fine-tuned every detail of the plan. Complex calculations, detailed simulations, and three-dimensional models became their daily routine. There was no room for error. The fate of humanity was at stake.

CHAPTER 38: THE SECRET AND THE FEAR

With the action plan ready, Selena and the scientists received a direct order: keep everything discovered in secrecy. The disclosure of the truth could trigger panic and unleash unnecessary chaos among the population. The burden of keeping that secret weighed on the shoulders of all the scientists. The information was restricted to a small group of specialists, protected by strict security measures. The researchers understood the fear and uncertainty that could arise if the general public knew the truth.

Selena, though aware of the importance of confidentiality, felt the emotional weight of the situation: the responsibility to safeguard humanity. It was April 26, 2022, and the Mexican scientists were immersed in the constant review of the data. The findings confirmed the concerns raised by King Pakal years ago. Time was an unrelenting enemy, but also an opportunity to find a solution.

After meticulous analysis, the scientists refined the plan and its possible solution: divert the trajectory of 2012 XE133 before it collides with Apophis. They knew it was a challenging task, but hope burned in their hearts. The mission had to achieve a deviation of at least one degree, and, even more crucially, it had to be accomplished four years in advance.

Bright minds set into motion, calculating and meticulously designing the plan to alter the course of the asteroid 2012 XE133. Every detail was essential; every calculation had to be precise. The collaboration between scientists and experts strengthened, sharing ideas, confronting hypotheses, and drawing from collective knowledge.

CHAPTER 39: THE ROCKET OF HOPE

April 28, 2022, with the certainty that they had a possible solution, the governments of the United States and Mexico decided to convene the United Nations (UN). The mission was to inform about the discovery and present the proposed measure to prevent the collision.

The meeting room was filled with representatives from different countries, all aware of the gravity of the situation. Selena, along with the Mexican scientists, presented the data and the strategy to impact the asteroid 2012 XE133 and divert its trajectory.

Silence invaded the room as the delegates absorbed the information. It was a race against time and uncertainty, but also an opportunity to demonstrate the unity and strength of humanity in adversity. The UN, aware of the urgency and the potentially disastrous consequences of the collision, unanimously approved the proposed measure.

With global support secured, an unprecedented alliance formed to face the cosmic challenge. Scientists, engineers, astronauts, and leaders from around the world joined forces in a mission of salvation. The objective was clear: impact the asteroid 2012 XE133 and alter its course, thus safeguarding Earth from an uncertain fate.

The countdown began. Hopes and fears intertwined, but the determination of humanity was unyielding. The future of Earth was at stake, and the courage and creativity of science and global cooperation would be put to the test.

On May 5, 2022, on a day filled with tension and hope, NASA prepared for the launch of the Pakal rocket. This rocket, named in honor of the Mayan king, carried a mission of vital importance: to alter the trajectory of the asteroid 2012 XE133 and thus protect Earth from the imminent collision with Apophis.

In the control center of NASA, the atmosphere was one of anticipation and determination. Scientists and astronauts had meticulously prepared for this crucial moment. The Pakal rocket, imposing on the launch platform, represented the last hope for humanity.

With a countdown, the timer reached zero, and the rocket majestically ascended into the sky. The deafening roar of the launch filled the air, while the hearts of those present beat with a mix of excitement and anxiety. The rocket carried a special payload: a nuclear bomb designed to alter the trajectory of the asteroid by a crucial degree.

CHAPTER 40: THE RENAISSANCE

On July 31, 2023, just over a year after the launch of the Pakal rocket, the long-awaited moment arrived. The rocket had reached the rendezvous point with the asteroid 2012 XE133. It was the moment of truth, the opportunity to change the fate of humanity.

With millimetric precision, the Pakal rocket approached the asteroid. The astronauts' pulses quickened as they prepared for impact. The spacecraft released the nuclear bomb, and it detonated with a brilliant explosion.

The flash of light spread in the vacuum of space, and the impact was a success. Asteroid 2012 XE133 deviated from its original course, moving farther away from the collision trajectory with Apophis. Earth had averted an imminent catastrophe.

A collective sigh of relief swept through the NASA control center, and applause and jubilation erupted. Hugs and tears of joy intertwined as the news of success spread worldwide. Humanity had faced its greatest threat and had prevailed.

However, there was a sense of humility and gratitude in victory. The reality of how close they had been to disaster was etched in collective memory. Unity and teamwork had saved Earth from a catastrophic fate.

This historic event demonstrated the power of science, global cooperation, and human resilience. The lesson learned would resonate with future generations, reminding them of the importance of protecting and preserving our fragile planet.

As cosmic dust dissipated, humanity looked to the future with renewed hope. They had bravely confronted danger and had triumphed.

It is October 14, 2023, the world is in a state of joy and gratitude for an annular solar eclipse visible at Chichen Itza. However, the vast majority is unaware that the catastrophe has been averted, and Earth has been saved from imminent danger. In the heart of Chichen Itza, one of the wonders of the ancient Mayan civilization, the celebration is in full swing due to the proximity of the inauguration of the most important engineering project in America, the Mayan Train.

The sky darkens slowly as the total solar eclipse unfolds before the amazed eyes of the gathered crowd. It is a symbolic moment, a resurgence of hope personified by Kukulkan, the feathered serpent of Mayan mythology, and people embrace and cry with joy, knowing that they have witnessed a transcendent moment in the history of humanity. Cheers and applause fill the air as the eclipse becomes a symbol of rebirth and overcoming adversity.

CHAPTER 41: A LEGACY OF JUBILEE

It's December 15, 2023, and Selena and Emmanuel, the brave scientists who played a crucial role in saving the world, are filled with joy and satisfaction. They have achieved the unimaginable and can now enjoy the peace and happiness they deserve.

Alongside them, the scientists who collaborated on the project come together in an unparalleled celebration—the inauguration of the Mayan Train. They laugh, toast, and share stories of the challenges overcome and moments of uncertainty. They know they have left an indelible mark on the history of humanity.

Meanwhile, the thousands of tourists visiting the Mayan area and its majestic ruins marvel at the greatness of the ancient civilization. Aboard the fabulous Mayan Train, a symbol of connection and discovery, and as passengers on the unit named after the Mayan King, Pakal, travelers explore archaeological sites, immersing themselves in the cultural richness and beauty of the region.

The experience is enriching, as people from all parts of the planet come together in fascination and respect for the history and wisdom of the ancient Maya. The remnants of the past become a reminder of the importance of protecting our heritage and valuing the fragility and beauty of our world.

The future is glimpsed with renewed hope. Humanity has proven its ability to face challenges and find solutions. Collaboration and perseverance have proven to be the most powerful tools in the fight for a better world.

As the sun shines over Chichen Itza and the Mayan Train advances through the vast Mayan land, an imposing monument has been erected to King Pakal at the entrance of the archaeological zone to bear witness to the foretelling of a great king, while the legacy of the ancient civilization lives in every human heart of those who inhabit the land of the Mayab.

History reminds us that, despite our differences, we all share the same home and a common responsibility: to protect and preserve our precious planet.

Selena, Emmanuel, and the scientists who starred in this extraordinary story have reached the end of their journey. Having fulfilled their mission to save the world, they now enjoy the moment in the beautiful southeast.

The tranquility of the region is a balm for their weary souls. They spend their days in the company of loved ones, savoring the serenity and beauty of the surrounding nature. They also organize talks for tourists visiting the Temple of the Inscriptions, the sacred place that encapsulates the memory of King Pakal and his brave feat, all while gazing at the majestic Mayan ruins with a sense of awe and gratitude, remembering the vital role they played in history.

CHAPTER 42: HOUSTON WE ARE IN TROUBLE

It's July 31, 2024, a warm summer day in Palenque, Chiapas. Selena and Emmanuel strolled among the majestic ruins of the Temple of the Inscriptions. The sun shone upon the ancient pyramids, and the air vibrated with the history of this mysterious Mayan city. Both were enjoying their long-awaited journey, marveling at the engineering and astronomical knowledge of this ancient civilization. However, something unexpected was about to interrupt their idyllic getaway.

While standing in front of the imposing Temple, a message on their mobile phones alerted them to shocking news: NASA had detected a change in the trajectory of the asteroid 1990 MU due to its collision with the asteroid 2012 XE133, altering its course and now on a collision course with Earth for the year 2027. This asteroid, the size of the Great Pyramid of Giza, has a diameter of about 200 meters.

As Selena and Emmanuel read more about the asteroid, the gravity of the situation became increasingly evident. The asteroid 1990 MU was traveling at an incredible speed, almost 30 kilometers per second. If it were to impact Earth, the damage would be devastating. The energy released at the moment of impact would be equivalent to the explosion of thousands of nuclear bombs. Entire cities could be wiped off the map, and the environmental consequences would be catastrophic.

Selena and Emmanuel, now overwhelmed by the news, walked in silence through the ancient archaeological site, their minds filled with worry, dismayed and with a sense of guilt. The awe-inspiring past of the Mayan culture seemed even more impressive when they realized the fragility of Earth in the vast cosmos. The ancient Mayan wisdom about the stars now took on a much deeper meaning as they realized something they hadn't taken into account when diverting the trajectory of asteroid 2012 XE133.

The city of Palenque lay silently under the stars, like a mute witness to the ancestral secrets that had been unveiled in the search for the Omen of King Pakal. Selena and Emmanuel had tirelessly traveled through three countries seeking answers in the codices and the hieroglyphs carved into the stone of their pyramids. The key to avoiding the catastrophe was buried in ancient history, but apparently, it had not been fully revealed yet.

Suddenly, Selena remembers that there is a piece they never investigated – the fourth codex referenced by King Pakal, to be written by the eldest descendant who survived after the impact of the first asteroid. Could this be the missing piece to decipher the enigma of King Pakal? Without this codex, the Mayan data they had left in their codices so far seemed sufficient to calculate the astronomical event foretold by King Pakal. However, after this chilling news, it appears that there is something more that they failed to consider.

Selena and Emmanuel sense that there is an essential piece in the puzzle left by the Mayans to fully understand the consequences of diverting the asteroid and the possible warnings from Pakal, as they never identified that there might be another asteroid involved, as is the case with 1990 MU.

The wind whispered through the ruins of Palenque, and the moon rose majestically in the sky. "We need to find the Fourth Codex, Emmanuel," said Selena, looking at the horizon with determination. "It's our last hope to tie up all the loose ends and prevent this catastrophe."

Emmanuel nodded, aware of the urgency of the situation. But as they continued their search, they recalled some surprising news: the Osiris spacecraft, which had collected samples from the Bennu asteroid in 2023 and was already on its way back to Earth, might have important data about the composition of asteroids that could help them avoid the collision of asteroid 1990 MU with the planet.

The news injected a new spark of hope into Selena and Emmanuel. Modern technology and ancient knowledge could finally come together to protect the planet. But the big question remained unanswered: would it be enough? Could they ultimately find the Fourth Codex before it's too late and discover some other data to prevent the catastrophe?

The Omen of King Pakal entered its final chapter, where the past and the future converged in a race against time. Humanity hung in a delicate balance, and the answer to the question that had been suspended throughout history remained an enigma. The search for the last piece of the puzzle was underway, and the fate of Earth was at stake.

Will Selena and Emmanuel decipher the enigma and, with the help of NAS scientists, prevent the apocalypse in time? Is it possible that the Maya left behind another astronomical detail that was overlooked in the calculations?

This story will continue...

APPENDIX 1: DEITIES

The Maya mythology includes a wide variety of deities, and the importance of these deities can vary depending on the regions and time periods. There is no clear consensus on which ones were the most important, as opinions may differ. Here I present to you the 40 Maya deities, without a specific order of importance, emphasizing that this list is not exhaustive and interpretations may vary. Additionally, some names may have regional variants or be known by different names in different Maya communities.

- Itzamná: God of the sky and creation.
- Kukulkán (Quetzalcóatl): Feathered serpent, god of knowledge and culture.
- Ixchel: Goddess of the moon, fertility, and medicine.
- Ah Puch: God of death and lord of the underworld.
- Chaac: God of rain.
- Hunab Ku: Supreme god, creator of the universe.
- Ixpiyacoc and Ixmucané: Divine couple, responsible for the creation of humanity.
- Ek Chuah: God of commerce and merchants.
- Yum Kaax: God of agriculture and harvest.
- Ixtab: Goddess of suicide and sacrifice.
- Yum Cimil: God of death.
- Gucumatz: Feathered serpent, creator and civilizing deity.
- Yumil Kaxob: God of hunting and nature.
- Bacabes: Four gods associated with the cardinal points, each with specific functions.
- Ah Mun: God of corn.
- Chac Chel: Goddess of the rainbow and sister of Ixchel.
- Ix Tabai: Goddess of harvest and fertility.
- Yum Nik: God of the wind.
- Cizin (Kisin): God of the earth and death.
- Ah Hulneb: God of medicine and herbs.
- Ah Tzul: God of fire.
- Bacab Kuk: God of wind and everyday life.
- Ah Hoya: Goddess of the moon.
- Ah Chuy Kak: God of cocoa and trade.

- Ixtabay: Goddess of the moon and gestation.
- Ah Wucil: God of dreams and visions.
- Yum Kakix: God of wind and storm.
- Ix Tun: Goddess of stone and vegetation.
- Ah Uuc Ticab: God of fire and light.
- Ix Chebel Yax: Goddess of textiles and dyeing.
- Ah Patan: God of medicine and herbs.
- Ah Kulel: Goddess of love and fertility.
- Chirakan-Ixmucane: Goddess of creation and procreation.
- Ah Kantenal: God of the sky and creation.
- Ix Uwa: Goddess of weaving and the moon.

APPENDIX 2: CALENDARS

The Maya culture used various calendars for different purposes. The three main calendars in Maya culture are:

Tzolk'in: Also known as the "sacred calendar" or "ritual calendar," the Tzolk'in is a cycle of 260 days composed of 20 periods or months of 13 days each. Each day has a unique combination of a number (from 1 to 13) and a name, which repeats after 260 days.

Haab: The Haab is the "solar calendar" or "civil calendar." It consists of 18 months of 20 days each, plus an additional month called Wayeb, which has only 5 days. In total, the Haab has 365 days, making it approximately equivalent to our solar year.

Long Count: The Long Count is a day-count system representing a continuous count of days from a mythological reference date. It is expressed in units called kin (days), uinal (20-day months), tun (years of 360 days), k'atun (20 years of 360 days), and b'ak'tun (400 years of 360 days). The Long Count can represent very large dates and is commonly used for historical dates and long-term astronomical events.

These three calendars operated in parallel and combined to form more complex dates. The combination of a Tzolk'in day with a Haab day results in a cycle of 18,980 days or 52 Maya years, known as the Calendar Round. Additionally, the Long Count was used for more extensive dates and continues to be used in archaeological and epigraphic studies to date monuments and significant events.

The Tzolk'in, or sacred calendar of the Maya, is composed of 20 periods or months of 13 days each. The periods of 13 days are called "Uinales" or "Winales."

Mayan names for the 20 periods or months of the Tzolk'in calendar:

- Imix (serpent)
- Ik (wind)
- Kan (crocodile)

- Akbal (night)
- Ix (woman)
- Men (monkey)
- Cib (reed)
- Caban (house)
- Etz'nab (flint)
- Cauac (storm)
- Ahau (lord)
- Chikchan (serpent)
- Cimi (death)
- Manik (hand)
- Lamat (jaguar)
- Muluc (water)
- Oc (dog)
- Chuen (monkey)
- Eb (earth)
- Ben (reed)

Mayan names for the 13 days of the Tzolk'in calendar:

- Kin (day)
- Chikchan (serpent)
- Cimi (death)
- Manik (hand)
- Lamat (jaguar)
- Muluc (water)
- Oc (dog)
- Chuen (monkey)
- Eb (earth)
- Ben (reed)
- Ix (woman)
- Men (monkey)
- Cib (reed)

This is the meaning of these Maya names:

- Imix: Sea serpent. Symbolizes creation, change, and duality.

- Ik': Wind. Symbolizes spirit, creativity, and communication.
- Ak'b'al: Darkness, night. Symbolizes introspection, mystery, and rebirth
- .K'an: Corn. Symbolizes abundance, nourishment, and life.
- Chikchan: Lizard. Symbolizes cunning, adaptation, and survival.
- Kimi: Death. Symbolizes transformation, the end of cycles, and new beginnings.
- Manik': Hand. Symbolizes skill, ability, and creation.
- Lamat: Jaguar. Symbolizes strength, power, and nobility.
- Muluk: Water. Symbolizes purification, fluidity, and life.
- Ok: Dog. Symbolizes loyalty, fidelity, and protection.
- Chuwen: Monkey. Symbolizes intelligence, cunning, and joy.
- Eb': Earth. Symbolizes stability, connection, and fertility.
- B'en: Reed. Symbolizes maturity, wisdom, and harvest.

These Maya names reflect the deep connection that the ancient Maya had with nature and the cosmos. Each name represents an essential force or characteristic of the universe, and the Maya believed that these names held real power in their lives.

CALENDARIO MAYA (FOTOGRAFIA DE RAFAEL PARRAO)

ADDITIONAL THANKS

The plot of this novel is the author's original idea. The texts were generated and translated into English with the help of an language model developed by Open AI called Chat GPT and customized by the author.

Some of the images were taken by the author with his camera, the rest of this work were designed using artificial intelligence through the Leonardo.ai application and are property of the author according to the terms of licensing paid for the use of said application.

Made in the USA
Columbia, SC
03 October 2024

42824998R00067